Power, passion, (
World that

A Very Proper Monster

In Victorian-era Dublin, Josephine Shaw spends long nights filling the pages of her Gothic stories with the fantastic and the macabre, unaware that the suitor her father has arranged is one of the dark creatures she's always dreamed. For Tom Dargin, courting an ailing spinster was only one duty in a long life of service to his sire. But after he meets the curious Miss Shaw, will Tom become the seducer or the seduced? Can a love fated to end in tragedy survive a looming grave?

A VERY PROPER MONSTER is an Elemental World historical novella originally published in the *Beneath a Waning Moon* gothic duology. This special stand-alone edition contains a bonus short story, *Night in the Waking City*.

Tom and Josie travel to New York City to meet with allies and publishers, but a chance encounter sends Josie into a rage, leaving Tom to look for unexpected allies in the city that never sleeps. Can a young human and an ancient vampire find his ailing mate before Josie does something she'll regret?

A Very Proper Monster
An Elemental World novella

With *Night in the Waking City*

Elizabeth Hunter

☩

For my writing friends

You know who you are

Girls are caterpillars when they live in the world, to be finally butterflies when the summer comes;
but in the meantime there are grubs and larvae...
each with their peculiar propensities, necessities
and structures.

—*Carmilla*
Joseph Sheridan Le Fanu

PROLOGUE

Dublin, 1886

My dearest Miss Tetley,

Enclosed you will find the final draft of Viviana Dioli's "The Countess's Dark Lover," a story within which you will no doubt find numerous additional faults. Signorina Dioli turns an indifferent profile to you, her harsh editor. I'm afraid she simply cannot find it in her cold heart to remove the balcony scene and subsequent mortal fall. Gothic romance, my dear Miss Tetley, so rarely comes to a happy end. And after all, what would be your actions when pursued by the grim monster which Warwick was revealed to be?

As for your other inquiries, rest assured I am no better or worse than when last I wrote. If I am completely honest, Lenore, I seem to be in some terrible stasis. The physicians know I am not so foolish as to hope for a cure, nor am I morbid enough to welcome my inevitable end peacefully. Part of me wishes that the sanatoriums they continue to suggest were possible, but I cannot bear the thought of leaving Father alone, even if I am ill.

So I trudge on, writing my stories, traveling to take the sea air when possible, and worrying about Father. No doubt you've heard of his own failing health. I know he wrote to your dear parents only last week, and I do hope he was frank. He is not well.

I have no worries about his businesses, for he has spent the past few years affixing the most competent men in positions of authority. But my own failing health, combined with his inevitable retirement, means that he does worry about the continuance of his legacy. Shaw mills have employed hundreds, but the boat works are poised to be entirely more impressive than the mills. And you know, for your father has the same honorable bent, how much the well-being of those many men and women weighs on his mind.

Would that I were a healthy son!

But alas, then I would have been forced to turn my head to business instead of literature of questionable moral value, and the world would have been robbed of Miss Dioli's and Mister Doyle's brilliance. (You know, of course, that I speak in false pride, for my own wit does amuse me too much.)

While I wish my cousin were of a mind to manage the businesses in good temper, I fear he is not. Neville eyes my every discreet cough with a kind of manic glee. Or is it my own morbid fascination that finds his expression so? I confess I am not impartial, having never liked the boy. I like even less the man he has become.

I do believe Father will seek to sell if his health shows no sign of improving. There are more than a few eager speculators, but he will sell only to someone who sees the boat works as he does. Not only industry, but the realization of a dream. If he could find an honorable benefactor to carry on his legacy, I believe he would happily sell.

For now, my dear Lenore, think of me and the dark depths of madness I must plumb to write this next horrible tale. I do say living in Miss Dioli's fanciful (if morbid) mind makes your friend a far pleasanter companion for poor Mrs. Porter. While Mr. Doyle's terrible imagination provides more pennies per word, he does take a terrible toll on the household staff. There will be no living with me, I am afraid, until this next monster has been exorcized on the page.

Wish me happy ink stains, Miss Tetley. No doubt you will see the beginnings of horror, though not the ghastly results, within the next fortnight.

Yours always,
Josephine Shaw

CHAPTER ONE

"THE MILLS AND THE BOAT works are both profitable," Tom Dargin said. "The business is well run, and his workers even like the man. Foremen have naught to say against him."

Tom waited as Murphy read the report Declan had drafted. Tom didn't want to rely on the numbers alone, but the report, combined with his own discreet inquiries about how Shaw ran his businesses, had led him to believe his sire was making the right move pursuing Shaw's boat works.

"I like all of this," Murphy said, raising his head. "The mills and the boat works *are* both profitable. So why are there rumors he's looking to sell?"

"Health," Tom said. "That's what some are speculating. He's gettin' on and his health isn't what it was. That's the rumor, anyway."

Murphy frowned. "And no children?"

"A daughter," Declan said. "Josephine Shaw. But she's consumptive. Rarely seen out in society, not for the past five years. There's a nephew, but they're not close."

"And a sick daughter means a son-in-law is hardly likely," Murphy mused, rubbing his chin. "Has he said anything publicly?"

"No," Tom said. "Though it seems pretty common knowledge among his foremen."

"Beecham's sniffing," Declan said. "As are a few human investors."

William Beecham, the vampire lord of Dublin, would be happy to pounce on the struggling company. They'd have to tread carefully.

"Has Shaw a manager?" Murphy asked.

"He did, but the man was hired away." Tom tried not to let the smile touch his lips. "I believe by one of Hamilton's works in Belfast."

"That bloody woman," Murphy said. "Why am I not surprised? At least it wasn't Beecham. Buying with a manager installed would be a hell of a lot easier."

"It would," Tom said, "but I can see two or more of the men I talked to rising to the position if given the proper incentive. Shaw hired lads for brains, not just strong backs."

"Smart," Declan said. "What do you think, boss?"

Murphy tapped his pen for a moment, fiddling with the new watch fob his mate, Anne, had given him. Tom wished the woman were there that evening, but she was visiting a friend in Wicklow that week. Murphy always made up his mind more quickly when Anne was around.

"He won't be going for money," Murphy said. "Or at least not only money. He has no son. He won't have any grandchildren. These businesses are his legacy."

"Agreed," Tom said. His sire could have acquired Shaw's assets through mental manipulation like many of their kind did. It was a point of honor for Murphy that he didn't and one of the reasons Tom had been so keen to join his former student in immortality.

A VERY PROPER MONSTER

It wasn't as if Patrick Murphy needed the old pugilist at his side for fighting advice anymore. But Murphy could be a little too trusting in Tom's opinion. He needed a bruiser at his back, and Tom had been happy to volunteer, even if it did mean having to feed on blood when the need arose.

He'd been a vampire for over thirty years, and all in all, it wasn't that bad. He missed the sun, but if he was honest, he'd been living the last years of his human life at night, hustling through Dublin and even over to London with Murphy, trying to scrounge enough money with boxing matches to make it worth the blood.

Now the blood came from donors, and Murphy was the one in charge. At least, that's what it looked like to outsiders. Murphy, Tom, and Declan presented themselves as brothers to mortal society. No one questioned their connection. In time they'd have to adjust, but for now it worked. Tom just had to remember to answer to "Mr. Murphy" on occasion.

"If Shaw is truly looking to sell, he will want someone who'll invest more than money," Tom said. "Someone who cares about the workers. That's my take, anyway."

"Agreed," Declan said.

"No harm in calling on the man," Murphy said. "We've already been introduced. Perhaps I come to him asking about improvements for my own millworks..."

Tom nodded. "Show him you're the kind who cares. A boss willing to invest for the long term."

Declan said, "Plus he might have something to help with the dust problem in Whitechurch."

"True." Murphy set his pen down. "Declan, write up

a letter, will you? Ask Shaw for a meeting next week if he's amenable. Let's see if John Shaw is a man willing to work with creatures of the night."

THE meeting had been six months coming, at least, and Tom had watched Shaw deteriorate in that time. The once-robust man had grown wan and pale as Tom and Murphy's respect for the human grew stronger.

"You know," Shaw said, "I spotted your intentions in our second meeting, Mr. Murphy."

Murphy smiled. "And yet you kept meeting me."

"It's the same kind of tactic I would have used when I was young," Shaw said with a drawn smile. "Of course I kept meeting with you."

Shaw was a hell of a businessman, but Tom approved of the core of honor in the man. When he'd been human, he would have felt privileged to work for a man like John Robert Shaw.

"And so," Murphy said more quietly, "we come to the sticking point. I want to buy the works, John. The mills and the boat works. You know that. What I need you to know is that it's not just about the money to me. I respect what you've done. I'm no Englishman to see only the profit in them. I see what the boat works have the potential to do for Dublin. For the whole of Ireland. That's important to me."

"I know." Shaw took a sip of his whiskey, and Tom noticed his hand trembling just a little. "I've made a study of you, young man. And while there are some... curious things rumored about you, I know a gentleman of good character when I see one. I like your wife. I like your brothers. You're a man who understands family."

Tom cocked his head. Shaw talked more than a little about family, which made the relative secrecy around his own something of a mystery. It was well-known he had a daughter, but Tom had never seen her. Neither had Murphy or Declan. She was a mystery. One that Tom Dargin couldn't help but wonder about.

"You're right. Family is very important to me," Murphy said.

"And me." Shaw dabbed at his brow. "I had this all planned, and now I find myself nervous to speak of it. Perhaps I'm absorbing some of Jo's fancy after all."

"Jo?" Tom asked from the settee.

Shaw had asked both Tom and Declan to join Murphy and him that night for a drink. Tom felt as he always did in company, like the prized ox accidentally let into someone's parlor. He was an unfashionably big man, and the scars on his face often led those in polite society to avoid his gaze. He was more at home with the factory workers than the bosses.

"My daughter, Josephine." Shaw took a deep breath. "As I imagine you have heard, she is not well. She has been unwell for years, despite the efforts of numerous physicians."

Tuberculosis, they called it now. Consumption, his mam had said. If the disease had progressed as far as rumors claimed, there would be no cure for Josephine Shaw, and Tom could see the knowledge in her father's eyes.

"Your own health...," Murphy said cautiously. "You fear you are deteriorating."

"I *am* deteriorating. And faster than my daughter.

She will be alone."

Tom knew Shaw was worried about his daughter's protection after he died. Those with consumption could linger for years. And while she might not hurt for money, a woman without a family to protect her was still at risk of being taken advantage of.

Murphy said, "Her family—"

"She has little to none. She has friends—good friends —but mostly in England where she went to school. Her cousin should be the one to care for her, but Neville has little interest in anyone but himself, and he will be furious when he learns I am looking to sell the businesses. He expects to inherit."

Tom's ears perked, and he made a mental note to keep an eye on this Neville. A disappointed would-be heir was nothing to trifle with. The quicker Shaw sold the whole works to Murphy, the better it would be for everyone. Let Neville become accustomed to disappointment while his uncle was alive to manage him.

"Mr. Shaw," Murphy said, "if you are concerned about your daughter, you needn't be. You have met my wife. Mrs. Murphy is a generous woman, both of heart and attention. And I'm sure Miss Shaw has inherited her father's good sense. My family would be happy to count your daughter a friend, as I have come to think of you as a fr—"

"She doesn't need a friend, she needs a husband," Shaw said abruptly.

The whole room fell silent.

Murphy stammered. "John... I say, I'm already married."

"And you've two brothers who aren't."

Tom glanced at Declan, whose eyes were the size of saucers. Declan knew Tom's taciturn demeanor and age hardly made him husband material, especially for a young woman not yet thirty. That left Declan the obvious choice, and he didn't look like he was jumping at the opportunity, even if the woman was an heiress.

Tom glued his lips shut. Let Murphy talk them out of taking on some consumptive spinster. He was the one with the silver tongue.

"John, wouldn't it be wiser to—"

"She doesn't think she needs a husband," Shaw said. "Has always resisted any attempts at matchmaking. Says she'd only be a burden. Foolish girl." Shaw's whole face softened. "She has been the delight of my heart. She deserves any happiness I can give her."

Murphy tread carefully. "If the young woman doesn't wish to be married," he said, "wouldn't it be more prudent to find a reliable companion for her as she declines? Anne's and my offer of friendship remains. We are more than willing—"

"If one of your brothers marries Josephine, it settles the whole business, don't you see?" Shaw said. "You will be *family*. There will be no one to contest your purchase. There will be no one to wrest Josephine's fortune from her if she takes a turn. An employee cannot protect her from unscrupulous relations, Mr. Murphy. You know that." Shaw's face grew even paler. "The moment I pass from this world, the vultures will circle, particularly my nephew."

"How sick is she?" Tom asked quietly. "I don't mean to be indelicate, sir, but you may be seeing too dire a circumstance. Your daughter could very well—"

"Her last doctor said she could expect two years. At the most." Shaw looked at Murphy, then at Declan sitting quietly beside him. "Two years, young man. Surely any honorable gentleman understands my concern as her father. It would be nothing to give her two years. She is educated. Independent. And when she passes—"

"Mr. Shaw," Declan interrupted. "While I am sure your daughter is a most agreeable young woman, I do not know her, nor does she know me. Surely she would not consent to this."

"She would if you charmed her," Shaw said. "As if all of Dublin doesn't know of the Murphy brothers' charm! Surely, Mr. Murphy, you could persuade her. I would not try to hide my machinations, of course. But she's a practical girl, my Jo." Shaw grimaced. "When she wants to be."

Tom's mind was racing. Courts could be unpredictable, especially when it came to issues of inheritance. Wills could be contested. And Beecham was always sniffing around Murphy, watching the younger vampire with jealous eyes. He would use any excuse—manipulate any connection—to thwart Murphy, though he couldn't do it openly.

Shaw was right. If Declan married the Shaw heiress, it would solve everything. Murphy would buy Shaw's businesses without argument. Shaw would be seen as handing over the reins to his daughter's new family. Not even Beecham would be able to manipulate Murphy's claim to the boat works.

And when the girl died... it wasn't as if she didn't have a fortune of her own. In a way, marriage to the

Shaw spinster would mean they were getting Shaw's businesses for little less than the cost of a wedding and care for a consumptive.

But Declan looked as if he were steps away from execution.

Ninny.

Murphy also saw the terrified look on his brother's face and leaned forward. "John, as much as I want to buy your factories, I cannot force my brother—"

"I'll do it," Tom said quietly. "If Miss Shaw would consent to marry me, I will wed her."

Wide eyes turned toward Tom.

"But only if she consents," he said again. "I won't force the girl or put up with having her coerced. From what you've said, Miss Shaw has little enough time left without her being miserable in a marriage she doesn't want."

Murphy's mouth was gaping open. Declan finally took a breath. And John Shaw was smiling.

"Good man," Shaw said.

Tom nodded, uncomfortable being the center of their attention. "Don't be too certain she'll accept me. She's the one who'll have to look at this ugly mug every night."

"Tom," Murphy said. "You don't have to do this. Shaw, I promise we will ensure your daughter—"

"It's little enough, Murphy." Tom glanced at Shaw, interrupting his sire before he could offend their host. "Little enough to ensure the protection of a young woman. I'm no prize. But if she'll have me, I'll have her."

Murphy looked at Tom a long time until Tom looked his sire in the eye and nodded. Murphy's shoulders relaxed and he turned to Shaw. "John, why don't you talk to your daughter first. We can wait to have my solicitor draw up the paperwork. Perhaps you could arrange a dinner sometime this week so my brother and your daughter could meet? I think we'd all like to meet Miss Shaw."

"CHRIST, Tom. Did you have to go and offer for the spinster?" Declan stormed into the room while Murphy and Tom were throwing back a pint of ale. Declan had stayed behind, talking to Shaw's family solicitor.

"Did you have to act like marrying the woman was such a torture?" Tom asked. "You'd have thrown the whole deal off with your clumsy excuses, Dec."

His brother pointed at him. "You've no business marrying the girl. Sure, we can fool Shaw and avoid the daylight when we do business with him, but have you thought about the consequences of trying to fool a wife? She'll have a staff. Servants. What the hell do you think you're going to do?"

"Be very careful," Murphy said. "This is Tom, Declan. Who's more careful than Tom?"

Tom didn't feel very careful, and for the first time in thirty years, he wished he could fall into the sweet oblivion liquor had once brought him and not just taste it. For the first ten years of immortality, it had haunted him. He still had all the same reasons to drink with none of the relief alcohol had once afforded.

When he'd finally turned his mind to controlling the baser urges that had driven him as a human, he'd found some peace. Now he was voluntarily taking on the care of a wife. A sick wife. He had no business taking care of anyone, much less a sick spinster.

Murphy looked at him with an expression that said he could hear all Tom's doubts rising to the surface. "It'll be fine, Tom," his sire said. "If you need to, you can touch her mind. Or have Anne do it. She has the most control."

"Jayzuz," Declan groaned. "What's Anne going to say? She'll have your head for this, Murphy."

"She'll not," Tom said. "I'm the one that put us all in this by offering. I'll tell Anne."

None of them wanted to anger Murphy's mate. She was the glue that held their small family together. But Tom knew she'd be keen to protect a vulnerable human woman, even if it meant inconvenience for the rest of them for a couple of years. Anne had a soft heart.

"I'm going out," Tom said, placing his glass carefully on the bar in Murphy's office.

"I saw some of Beecham's crew on the way here," Declan said. "Be careful. They're sniffing."

Murphy had taken the space near the docks because Beecham never dirtied his fine leather shoes by the waterfront. Their crew could operate with some amount of discretion there away from the finer eyes of Dublin immortal society and the corruption of its lord.

And Tom's upcoming marriage might blow that all to hell.

"Don't think of it," Murphy said, reading Tom's mind. "We always knew we'd attract attention with a move to take over Shaw's boat works. There was no avoiding this. Marriage to the Shaw girl won't make that any better or worse."

Declan shrugged. "At least she's not popular in society. She won't have to explain your lack of social graces. I inquired discreetly after you both left. The woman is practically an invalid. Twenty-eight years old, but her health started failing soon after she came out in society. Most of her education was in England. She maintains correspondence but hardly leaves the grounds unless she's going to their house by the sea for her lungs. Very few callers. No one mentioned her looks, which means she's plain. Probably dim too. Otherwise she'd have an offer of marriage, even if she was on the edge of death, solely for her fortune." Declan laughed. "Probably more than one."

"She went to school," Tom said, already feeling protective of the lady. "I highly doubt any daughter of Shaw's is a dullard. Besides that, how do you know she hasn't had an offer? Shaw said she never wanted a husband. Said she was 'independent.'"

He found himself admiring her for it, even though *independent* might be polite society code for foolish and stubborn. As long as the girl had her wits, Tom wouldn't be miserable. He could respect a stubborn woman. He was no pushover himself.

"Why don't we all withhold judgment until we've met the woman?" Murphy said. "If she's anything like her father, I expect she and Tom will get along well. The details can be worked out in time. Tom, take your walk if you've a mind, but keep an eye out for Beecham's lads."

"Will do, boss."

Tom left the warehouse, slipping down the back alleys along the river and heading south toward the Shaws' fine house on Merrion Square. He had a mind to watch it. Why? He didn't exactly know.

He wasn't in any kind of rush, so he stretched the walk out for an hour or so, plenty of time for most of the city to fall asleep. Tom liked the silence. He was a quiet man and always had been, even in human life. It was hard enough to avoid gathering notice when you were over six feet tall and built like a brick wall, as his mam had told him. He was only ever going to be a brute with size like that.

It was pure luck he'd fallen into boxing as a human. More luck that when his own body had started to give out, he'd run into a brash young Traveller who needed coaching and a companion to watch his back. Tom Dargin had thrown in with Murphy within weeks of meeting the young man, seeing in him the kind of luck Tom had always admired but never captured.

And now he'd be marrying a proper society woman if that woman would have him.

Wasn't life unexpected?

He lurked across the way from the Shaw house, surprised by the number of lights still on inside. Comfortable in the shadows, he crossed the main thoroughfare on the north side of the square and walked down a side street, curious to see if the Shaws' garden was accessible. He wanted to know who was awake. Who would be using gas lamps so late at night? Surely not one of the servants. Was it old Mr. Shaw himself, worried about his company and his failing health? Or perhaps it was Miss Shaw, unable to sleep or discomforted by her illness.

Either way, Tom was curious. And a curious Tom was a stubborn thing.

He walked across the muddy road behind the house where delivery carts had left deep grooves in the mud. A light mist was falling, and he drank it in, replete with the surge of power it lent his amnis. Unlike Murphy, who preferred fresh water, Tom felt most at home near the sea. But any water would do. He'd never been a particular man.

Following the lights led him past numerous walled gardens until he finally arrived at the back side of the stately redbrick Georgian home belonging to John Robert Shaw. It was handsome but not ostentatious. Respectable but not ancient. He'd watched Shaw exit the front of the house on more than one night, but he'd never investigated the gardens. Declan might have looked through the Shaw books, but it was Tom who gathered information on the ground.

That night, Tom Dargin scaled the garden wall and dropped into another world.

Far from the well-tended, orderly garden he'd imagined from Shaw's tidy appearance, this garden was a wild tangle of trees and flowers. Statuary hid among rocks tumbled artfully around the bases of trees, giving the dark garden a fantastical appearance. A miniature glass house lit up the center of the lawn, sparkling from the inside with candlelight. Tom felt as if he'd slipped into one of the fairy stories his grandmother had been fond of telling.

For standing in the center of a lush lawn, dressed in a white dressing gown, was a tall woman, as willowy as the trees that lined the garden. She stood, swaying a little, her pale skin touched by the moon's silver light as she held a book in her hand and turned in place. Her feet were bare, her dark hair fell past her waist, and her long gown was drenched in the evening dew.

It must be Miss Shaw. No servant would take a book out into the garden in the middle of the night. Certainly not in their dressing gown.

"'But dreams come through stone walls...'" She held up the book to the moon's light and spoke quietly, though his immortal hearing could pick up the words easily. "'...light up dark rooms, or darken light ones, and their persons make their exits and their entrances as they please, and laugh at locksmiths.'"

She twirled on the lawn, lifting the book over her head and humming a tune as her hair lifted while she spun.

"Dreams come through stone walls...," she whispered into the night as Tom watched from the dark shelter of a drooping willow.

"Oh, feck me," he muttered under his breath, letting out a sigh. "She's mad as a March hare."

CHAPTER TWO

JOSEPHINE ROBERTA DOYLE SHAW was a practical woman. Despite her rather eccentric writings, she ran her father's household with quiet efficiency, though she was wise enough to bow to the expert opinion of Mrs. Morse, the housekeeper her mother had hired before her untimely—and, Josephine preferred to think, tragic—death. As her mother had died in childbirth, Josephine had never felt her loss, though she liked to imagine she and her mother would have been the closest of confidantes and the dearest of friends.

As it was, Eloisa Shaw had left her daughter with an excellent and loving nanny, an efficient housekeeper, and an extensive and not-at-all proper library with books in Italian, French, and Spanish, as well as all the more conventional writings. This had motivated Josephine to excel early in languages, and by the time she was thirteen, she could explore the forbidden tomes her mother had left behind.

Josephine had not been disappointed.

As well as firing her imagination in very improper ways, her mother's own notes in the margins of the most scandalous books gave Josephine a peek into the mind of the woman she must have been.

A VERY PROPER MONSTER

Which was why when she embarrassed her father—as she inevitably did—Josephine reminded him that he had been the one to marry Eloisa Francesca Dioli Doyle in the first place. Therefore, if any scandal resulted from her reading Italian romances and French philosophy, it was entirely his own fault.

She was sitting in her library when her father presented his latest idea to ensure her future.

"You want me to *what*?" she said, laughing lightly so as not to provoke her lungs. "Marry him? One of your business partner's brothers?"

He leaned toward her, her gentle father who had always indulged her every whim. If she were a petulant child, he would have ruined her. Luckily, Josephine was eminently good-natured and had been blessed with a very strict nanny.

"Jo, you know you must."

"No, I don't know I must. Father, in addition to the rather large fortune you have worked very hard for, I also have my own income, modest though it may be. I will never be destitute. You are fretting for nothing."

"And when I die? When your cousin tries to take the house?"

She shrugged. "He could try. But if you should pass before me—though I think you are not quite as ill as you imagine—I will sell the house to some eager buyer with Mr. Macon's help, then I shall take Mrs. Porter and Mrs. Morse with me to the house in Bray. You know I don't like society." She let a sad smile touch her lips. "And you know it will not be for long. I am happy as I am."

"But if you were married..." He sighed. "Jo, I would worry so much less."

"I know."

The soft pang in her chest was not only from the tuberculosis that plagued her. For though Josephine Shaw was a practical woman, she also had the fiery heart of a romantic. It wasn't that she'd never longed for love. She had. When she was younger, she'd longed most desperately! But she'd known by the age of twenty-three that her health was becoming more and more fragile. And by twenty-five that the doctors' treatments would not save her life. It seemed cruel to hope for any happiness besides her own small fancies.

She wrote her stories, and they were read and enjoyed—or so Lenore claimed—by many. Josephine enjoyed quiet society and music and books and gardening. She loved her father to distraction.

It was with that love in mind that she took his hand. "Father, I promise I will be fine."

She tried to ignore the tears in the corners of his eyes when he squeezed her hand tightly.

"You deserve much more than 'fine,' my dear girl. You deserve a love like your mother and I had. I only had her for four years, but it has been enough to sustain me for twenty-nine."

"And do you think I will find love in an arranged marriage?" She had to smile. "You cannot make a young man love me because you do. I do not think that is the way love works."

"If he only meets you, he will have to love you."

"Oh, Papa!" Josephine laughed harder, and she couldn't stop the cough that followed. She muffled it in the handkerchief Lenore had embroidered for her. No blood—thank God—yet. "I think you are biased in my favor, but I will take the compliment. Surely Mr. Murphy will love me on sight. But shall I love him? This young man who would agree to a marriage to seal a business deal for his brother? No doubt he sees in our marriage a way to make his own fortune. Not that I begrudge ambition, but it doesn't lend itself to romance, does it?"

Shaw looked thoughtful. "If it was Declan Murphy, I might say you have the right of it, my dear. But it is not. Mr. Thomas Murphy, the oldest of the brothers, has offered for you."

"The oldest, is it?" Josephine quipped. "Well then, I might have a chance to outlive him after all."

Her father was abashed. "Not as old as that. But he is... a mature man. Perhaps in his forties. Not overly talkative. Not a pretty fellow at all, I suppose. Though I've noticed the serving girls all take note of him."

Josephine nodded solemnly. "I do bow to the measured opinion of observant serving girls when I consider suitors."

Shaw let go of her hand and leaned back, crossing his legs and brushing a hand over his trouser leg. "You're teasing your father."

She smiled. "It's just so silly. Why do I have need of a husband?"

"To protect you."

"I can protect myself. Or set the dogs on the marauders if they ignore my shrill and desperate cries."

His lips twitched with a smile. "To make you happy."

"You have no guarantee this Thomas Murphy is capable of that."

"Fine." He took her hand again. "To give your poor papa a measure of peace that I will leave you secure. I don't have long, Jo. I know that. If the Tetleys lived in Dublin, I would have no worry in your situation, for I know Margaret and Daniel love you as their own. But they do not live here, and you are not well enough to travel so far. All I am asking is that you give this man a chance to win your regard."

Josephine paused, persuaded by her father's worried pleas. "Very well, I will meet him."

"That is all I am asking."

"But if he thinks this union is somehow assured—"

"Mr. Murphy specifically said he would have you *only* if you would have him. He was quite clear that any kind of coercion on my part was unacceptable."

"Oh." That was... rather thoughtful. "I appreciate his regard in that matter."

"Meet him, Jo. You never know. Thomas Murphy may not be one of your romance heroes, but you might find him far more to your liking than you expect."

My dearest Miss Tetley,

You will be most astonished to find not only the pages of Mr. Doyle's latest horror enclosed, but also news of an even more alarming nature.

Father has found a gentleman to marry me!

I know you will be as dismayed as I am, dear Lenore. For herein lies the ruin of our plans in joint spinsterhood. I doubt my domineering (for surely he must be very domineering) future husband will consent to our scandalous plans to run away to the seaside and live out our lives wearing pantaloons.

A VERY PROPER MONSTER

Alas, no doubt the rogue will lock me in a tower or an attic until I wither away from disappointed love. With my fortune, he will have ample funds to find an appropriate tower or attic within easy distance of town as he is also a man of business and must surely not neglect his familial responsibilities.

I jest, of course. I have only allowed that I will meet Mr. Thomas Murphy, and Father has made every concession to my consent in the matter. I have no cause to presume lack of character in the gentleman, though the housemaids have rumored a rather hopeful and frightening scar on one side of his face. Further portent of illicit intent? Or perhaps a mere carriage accident in childhood? You know which one I would prefer, of course.

Father's health continues to fail. He is wracked with worry, which is the only reason I have consented to meet Mr. Murphy. I very much doubt a sick spinster of eight and twenty will tempt him, but as he has given his word to offer, it seems the engagement is mine to refuse. I will determine the truth in the man's face and decide my course. If he is a kind sort of man whose company I could endure, perhaps the engagement will give Father some comfort and me some amusement.

I long, my friend, though I dare not hope. You know that for which I have always wished. Perhaps fate is just cruel enough to see me madly in love before I die.

For I will die. You and Mrs. Porter will accuse me of consorting with the fairies, but I know it. I feel it in the night. I can feel Death's footsteps stalking me at the edges of the wild, and more and more, I find I do not want to run. I hope I will welcome him when he comes. Perhaps, in that pale lover, I will find the satisfaction that has so long eluded me in life.

Of course, I could also fling myself from the tower window in the midst of a violent thunderstorm. That would have more dramatic impact.

Your faithful (and sadly doomed) friend,
Josephine Shaw

SHE couldn't sleep, but then, did she ever sleep? Except for some lazy afternoons, Josephine had always been a restless creature, especially at night. By her calculations, if she slept only half as long as the average person, her life would not be cut in half. Merely... a third at the most.

She took an oil lamp to the garden and hid in the small glass house their gardener, Mr. Connelly, had built for her when she had returned from school. It was supposed to be for delicate plants, but it had become, much to no one's surprise, her own private study. Josephine didn't store her manuscripts in the glass house because she worried about the damp. But she often wrote there late into the night, the reflection of the lamp on the glass casting eerie shadows around her writing desk.

Josephine had never needed sleep to dream.

That night, she was neglecting her pen in favor of

rereading one of the most-favored books in her library. It was a small volume that had appeared mysteriously when she was only fifteen. Josephine still had no idea who had gifted her the lovely horror of *Carmilla*, but she owed her nameless benefactor an enormous debt. Her personal guess was a briefly employed footman who had seen her reading her mother's well-worn copy of *The Mysteries of Udolpho* and confessed his own forbidden love of Poe.

The slim volume of Le Fanu's Gothic horror stories had been hidden well into adulthood. As it wasn't her father's habit to investigate her reading choices, concealment might have been more for dramatic effect than real fear of discovery.

Josephine read by lamplight, curled into an old chaise and basking in the sweet isolation of darkness as she mouthed well-loved passages from her favorite vampire tale.

> *"For some nights I slept profoundly; but still every morning I felt the same lassitude, and a languor weighed upon me all day. I felt myself a changed girl. A strange melancholy was stealing over me, a melancholy that I would not have interrupted. Dim thoughts of death began to open, and an idea that I was slowly sinking took gentle, and, somehow, not unwelcome possession of me."*

She slammed the book shut.

How had she turned so morbid?

For while Josephine had long known she would not live to old age, she thought she had resigned herself to it. She made a point of fighting the melancholy that threatened her. If she had any regret, it was that she would not live long enough to write all the stories she wanted. Sometimes she felt a longing to shout them into the night, offering them up to any wandering soul that they might be heard so they could live.

So many voices beating in her chest. So many tales to write and whisper and shout. Her eyes fell to the book she'd slammed shut.

> *"You are afraid to die?"*
> *"Yes, everyone is."*

Josephine stood and pushed her way out of the glass house, into the garden where the mist enveloped her. She lifted her face to the moon and felt the tears cold on her cheeks.

"'Girls are caterpillars,'" she whispered, "'when they live in the world, to be finally butterflies when the summer comes; but in the meantime there are grubs and larvae, don't you see?'"

But the summer would never come for Josephine. She beat back the despair that threatened to envelop her.

You are afraid to die?

Yes, everyone is.

She lifted her face and opened her eyes to the starry night, speaking her secret longing into the night. "'But to die as lovers may—to die together, so that they may live together.'"

How she longed for love! For passion. How she ached to be seen. To be cherished. To be *known*.

She could pour her soul onto the page and still find loneliness in the dark. She strangled her heart to keep it alive, knowing it was only a matter of time until the palest lover took her to his bosom. Already, she could feel the tightness in her chest.

Tomorrow would not be a good day.

Nevertheless, she lifted her arms like an offering to a pagan god. "'Thus fortified I might take my rest in peace,'" she said, lifting her voice in defiance of the darkness. "'But dreams come through stone walls, light up dark rooms, or darken light ones, and their persons make their exits and their entrances as they please...'" She smiled. "'And laugh at locksmiths...' because they are clever dreams."

The sound of quiet laughter drifted through the garden.

She spun and glared into the darkness. "Who is there?" Josephine gathered her dressing gown, wrapping it closer around her body. "Who are you?"

Surely only a neighbor's servant, gawking at her foolishness. She should have been embarrassed, but she wasn't. She knew the neighbors considered her eccentric. It was the privilege of the dying.

"If you're going to spy on me"—Josephine stepped toward the bushes—"you will only see folly."

"I saw no folly tonight," a quiet voice replied. "Only perhaps a bit of fancy."

The voice was low and rough, coming from the edge of the garden. A man's voice, not a boy's. Coming from the other side of the wall? She couldn't tell for certain. But whoever was watching her, she didn't sense him moving away.

"Are you planning to kidnap me?" She cocked her

head, stepping closer to the edge of darkness. "I'll warn you, I'm consumptive. I'll probably make you sick if you try."

"My kind don't fall ill easily."

She froze. "Your kind?"

"Who were you talking to? The moon? God? Perhaps the fairies?"

"None of them, I think. Death, maybe."

He sounded amused when he said, "'Tis a foolish woman who courts Death. He is the most jealous lover."

Josephine stopped at the edge of the grass, not wanting to discover his secret. Whoever he was—servant or tramp, beggar or gentleman—she didn't feel fear. He had *heard* her, and she was grateful.

Josephine offered a sad smile into the shadows. "As I don't have any other lover, I suppose Death can have me."

She thought he came closer, though she had no idea why.

"Are you afraid to die?" her shadowed friend asked.

"No."

He waited.

"Yes," she whispered into his silence. "Everyone is."

A silent pause, then a murmur so close she felt his breath on her neck.

"Goodnight, Josephine."

But when she spun around, he was gone.

CHAPTER THREE

GIRLS ARE CATERPILLARS when they live in the world...

Tom tried not to fidget in the carriage on the way to Shaw's town house. Girls might be caterpillars according to Miss Shaw, but Tom felt like he was the one wrapped in a cocoon. The amount of clothing he'd been forced to don was verging on torture.

Normally he'd be able to get by with a more casual suit, even when socializing among Murphy's cronies. Tom Dargin hardly spoke. He was known as the stern older brother with dubious connections and a noted air of violence. Gentlemen respected him, greeted him properly if they met at clubs, but kept their distance.

Unfortunately, his sire's mate and valet had gotten ahold of him and forced Tom into his most formal attire.

He was miserable.

"You look very handsome," Anne said, leaning forward. "Please stop fidgeting."

"I'm a league off of handsome, Annie. And I'm not fidgeting."

"You've nearly torn the hem of that waistcoat. And if you cross your arms again, you're liable to tear the seams of that coat across the shoulders. Relax."

Relax? Tom had faced monsters in the boxing ring that unnerved him less than the thought of meeting a proper lady like Josephine Shaw. Especially when he already knew what the woman looked like in her dressing gown.

Did it bother him that his possible betrothed might be slightly insane? He hadn't quite decided yet. He thought probably not. Some of the most interesting people he'd known were a bit gone in the head, and he'd hardly be bored with her should she decide on him.

What he didn't like was that the decision was entirely in Josephine Shaw's hands. He'd promised to offer for the woman *if she wanted him*. Oddly enough, the thought that she might not was what made him worry his waistcoat. Because—and this had kept him pacing for three nights—Miss Shaw had surprised him by being entirely more desirable than anticipated.

"We're here."

Murphy's words pulled him from his mental dithering. The carriage jerked to a halt and the door opened. Tom had to stop himself from exiting first and looking around for threats. This wasn't a meeting with Beecham where vampires might be waiting with swords. This was a civilized dinner party with Murphy's mate, his new business partner, and a woman who ran around in her garden in the middle of the night quoting morbid poetry.

"Feck me," Tom muttered as he disembarked from the carriage. Murphy and Anne were waiting at the foot of the stairs. Declan—the sorry little ninny—had begged off.

Anne scowled. "You absolutely must not use

language like that in front of Miss Shaw."

"She might like it," Tom said. "You'd be surprised at the ladies who do."

Murphy covered a smile with cough and put his arm out for Anne. "Come now, Anne. Tom knows how to speak with a lady."

"No, I don't."

"And he'll even use a knife and fork when it's necessary," Murphy said.

"I promise not to stab anyone unless they try to steal my food," Tom added.

Anne shook her head. "I don't know why I put up with you scoundrels."

Murphy leaned closer to his mate and whispered something that would have made Tom blush if he could.

"Oh," Anne said in a slightly higher voice. "Yes, that's why. Well, God help Miss Shaw anyway if she likes you, Tom. I know you're as bad as this one, if not worse."

"Not our Tom," Murphy said. "He's the boring, responsible brother."

"I'd punch you, boss, but I might bust my seams," Tom said. "Come on now. Let's stop stalling." He could already see the butler waiting at the door.

They walked up the ruthlessly neat steps to the redbrick town house with tall glowing windows. Thank heaven the sun was setting earlier this time of year, otherwise they'd have to make excuses about the dinner hour.

The butler took Tom's hat and overcoat at the door before he led him, Murphy, and Anne back to the drawing room and announced them.

A rush of voices surrounded them, but Tom's eyes

found his target immediately. She was standing awkwardly near the bookcases, next to an older woman who looked like a companion. He could see a hastily set-aside book on the small table next to the lamp. Josephine Shaw was brushing at her skirts and slouching slightly, as if trying to conceal her height.

"And Mr. Murphy"—Tom blinked when he realized Shaw was speaking to him—"allow me to introduce you to my only daughter, Miss Josephine Shaw."

Tom stepped toward her.

Girls are caterpillars...

No girl here, but Tom thought he saw the caterpillar. Miss Shaw was... not pretty, though he thought she might be what some would call handsome. What had suited the darkness and moonlight appeared awkward in the artificial light of the drawing room. Her skin was pale, not luminous. Her hair was mouse-brown and tied back in a complicated, heavy knot. Her height and dramatic features were not flattered by the fashions she'd been buttoned into. But her eyes...

Too big for her face. Too dark. Too wide. Too... much.

Far too much for a very proper drawing room.

Tom thought her eyes might trap him if he wasn't careful.

"Miss Shaw." He bowed respectfully. "A pleasure to meet you."

Wake up, caterpillar.

She smiled politely and inclined her head, her shoulders still bent. Tom watched her ink-stained hand as he straightened, imagining what the skin would feel like in his rough palm. He stretched his shoulders back.

A VERY PROPER MONSTER

Those large, dark eyes that had been hovering somewhere around his cravat rose and kept rising to meet his own gaze.

"I find," he said quietly, "that it's quite useless to apologize for how tall the good Lord made me."

She blinked. "Pardon me, sir?"

He liked her voice even more when it wasn't whispered in a garden. And Anne would probably thrash him for it, but he'd say it anyway. "No need to slouch, Miss Shaw. In my opinion, there's nothing grander than a tall woman."

Miss Shaw blinked again. Then her face lit with a smile, she threw back her shoulders and let out a laugh as improper as dancing in the garden at midnight.

The laugh transformed her.

The older woman behind Miss Shaw met his eyes with an approving look, and Shaw clapped him on the shoulder as Miss Shaw continued to laugh.

"You young people," Shaw said. "Mr. Murphy, I have a good whiskey I've opened for the evening. May I get you a glass?"

"Please," Tom said. "And what are you drinking tonight, Miss Shaw?"

An attractive flush lent a little color to her face. "I rarely drink spirits, sir. I only take a bit of wine as my doctor recommends."

He liked that she made no pretense of hiding her disease.

Tom led Miss Shaw away from the bookcases and toward the fireplace where he found a seat for her near the cheerful hearth. She introduced Mrs. Porter, her companion, and asked him all the proper questions a young lady asks a young man of trade. Tom answered, even though he was far from a young man of trade.

It was very, very awkward.

"Tell me, Mr. Murphy, do you enjoy working with your brothers?"

He'd been watching the fire and thinking about how long it would be before dinner, so the answer slipped out before he thought. "Better than a team of asses, but not by much."

He heard Miss Shaw stifle a snort and barely contain a spit of wine that would have sprayed over her lovely green frock. Mrs. Porter's mouth hung open a little, though her eyes were alight in amusement.

"Bollocks," Tom muttered before he pressed a knuckle to his lips and tried not to growl. *Language, man. Watch your language.* "My sincerest apologies, Miss Shaw. I am too accustomed to the company of men. Please forgive my vulgarity."

Her voice was low and conspiratorial as she leaned toward him slightly. "I accept your apology. I hate dinner parties. Would you like to know why?"

"Yes."

"Because it takes five times as long to say something in polite language as it does by being forward. And all the really good jokes are forbidden."

"Don't you believe in manners, Miss Shaw?" He let the corner of his mouth turn up. "Are you trying to shock me?"

"I have a strong inclination that it would take quite a lot to shock you, Mr. Murphy."

"You might be correct."

If their self-appointed matchmakers were watching,

Tom thought they would probably be cackling with glee. Miss Shaw leaned toward him and he toward her. He couldn't help it. Something about her nature spoke to him. She was, despite her proper upbringing, an outsider by nature and circumstance. A caterpillar in a world that was not ready to see the butterfly she might become.

Tom wanted to see it.

He could smell the scent of gardenia in her hair and india ink on her fingers. And layered beneath that, he realized with an unexpected pang of sorrow, was the smell of her sickness. Of tonics and herbs she probably took to let her breathe easier.

"Miss Shaw, may I call on you tomorrow evening?"

She smiled, a sweet, cheerful expression with no artifice at all. "I would like that. I think... you and I might get on very well, Mr. Murphy."

THEY toasted him later, Murphy and Anne and Declan, who had miraculously appeared once Tom hadn't bollixed the whole affair.

"To Tom!" Murphy crowed. "Who knew a charming gentleman lurked beneath that ugly exterior?"

"Fuck off." Tom took a hearty drink of his ale and managed not to toss his sire into the wall.

Anne's eyes were sparkling. "I liked her. Very much. She's delightful, Tom. Pleasant, mature, and sensible."

Tom would have listed "sensible" fairly far down on the list of Miss Shaw's attributes. Anne's recitation of her virtues made Josephine Shaw sound dull. And the woman was anything but dull. But then, Tom had seen Miss Shaw running around the garden in her

37

nightclothes and Anne hadn't. That probably influenced his impression of her.

Anne continued to rave. "She's very intelligent. She seems a voracious reader, and she speaks six languages. Can you imagine? Six! English, Irish, French, Latin, Greek, and Italian. Her great-grandmother was Italian. I think her mother's family were all quite artistic. What fun company she will be!"

Italian, eh? That might explain her fairy eyes. But good Lord, how could Tom possibly keep the interest of a woman who spoke six languages? He barely spoke one.

"You know," Declan said, "if you wore that fancy getup out more, I think the ladies would be a bit keener on you, old man. Something about a rough-looking bloke in a suit."

"Tom doesn't need to worry about all the ladies," Anne said. "Only one for right now. And Miss Shaw could barely keep her eyes off him."

"Oh really now?" Tom tried not to squirm. "Well, she seems a nice enough girl."

"She's *not* a girl," Murphy said thoughtfully. "She's a smart, intelligent woman. I think she's appeasing her father with this whole business, because I felt no sense of the desperate spinster about her."

Tom nodded. "Agreed. She is very independent."

"She may like Tom," Anne said. "But do you think she'd marry him? And if she doesn't, will Shaw still follow through on the contract?"

"I think he'll follow through, but it would leave room for his relations to challenge in the courts if we don't have any family connection," Declan said. "The nephew, Neville Burke, could be problematic."

Murphy shrugged. "Does he have any influence? Any political allies we're unaware of?"

"He has Beecham," Declan muttered.

Tom sat up straight. "He has who?"

"Beecham." Declan raised his hand when Murphy started to speak. "I know. I discovered they've developed an acquaintance only tonight."

"Damn," Anne said quietly. "So much for Beecham not noticing this deal."

"There was never any real question of that," Murphy said as he sat next to his mate. He took her hand, kissing it absently. "We knew he'd not be able to ignore me once I made my move with Shaw. Once I buy Shaw's boat works, I'll control more jobs on the waterfront than he does. A good third, even counting the humans. There was no way that crazy old bastard wouldn't notice."

Tom asked, "Dec, did he have any acquaintance with Neville Burke before now? Any history of business with the man?"

"Not that I could find. According to Burke's driver, they've only been socializing for the past month or so."

"But often?"

Declan nodded and Tom scowled. Suddenly, romancing Josephine Shaw had taken on an entirely new urgency. If Beecham was cultivating a friendship with the human, it could only be because he saw some vulnerability in Murphy and Shaw's alliance.

An even more alarming thought struck him. "Murphy, do we have guards around the Shaws' home?"

"No." Murphy shook his head. "I didn't think it was necessary."

"It is." Tom stood up and walked toward the door.

"I'll take care of it. Right now."

All Tom could picture was Josephine dancing in the garden under the moonlight. She was as vulnerable as a babe. Anything could happen to her. Violence. Vampire influence. Hell, she'd been chatting with him in the shadows as if she hadn't a care in the world only three nights before.

Well, Tom decided, proper lady or not, Josephine Shaw would be getting a few more guards, and they'd be the most vicious lads he could find. No one, save him, was touching her.

TOM spotted her assigned guards the next night when he called on Miss Shaw. The two humans nodded at him, then went back to chatting behind newspapers as they waited in the square. He knew two more guards would be concealed in the garden behind the house, including a young vampire from Cornwall who'd come under Murphy's aegis only two years before.

She was a merciless little bit of an earth vampire whose lover was originally from Dublin. Kerra looked like a waif. If any of the humans spotted her, they'd likely try to feed her and give her a hand-me-down coat, not knowing she could tear their throat out before they'd have time to scream. She was the perfect guard for his woman.

He knocked on the door, a slim book he hoped Miss Shaw would like clasped in his hand, and the solemn butler ushered him into the gaslit entryway. He could hear voices coming from down the hall before he took off his hat.

"...know his supposed interest is only about your money, cousin."

"And I'm sure your interest is purely familial."

"I'm your cousin. I care about you."

A wry laugh. "It's almost as if you think I've forgotten all your slights over the years."

"Josephine—"

"Don't insult my intelligence, Neville. We both know you're angry that you won't inherit my money if I marry. Let me enlighten you: you wouldn't have inherited anyway. My will is something I saw to years ago. So whatever happens between me and Mr. Thomas Murphy, you can be assured my fortune—and father's—is well out of your reach."

Tom put a hand on the butler's arm, holding him back from announcing his presence. The butler, who was obviously not a fool, nodded silently. Tom waited outside the library, curious what Neville Burke's response would be.

"You're a foolish girl, Jo. And wills, especially those made by sick old spinsters, are always subject to interpretation. I have friends who can be very influential."

Jo. It was a darling nickname, but Tom didn't like the cousin using it. Neville Burke should only call her Josephine, if he had to speak to her at all.

"I am not a girl. Nor am I foolish. But you *are* foolish if you think you've hired better attorneys than mine. Good-bye, Neville. I'm expecting company, and I don't want you around. Is that plain enough language for you? And don't bother my father again. Make no mistake: I run this household, and you are not welcome in it unless you have an invitation."

Tom nodded at the butler, who knocked a second before he pushed the door open.

"Mr. Thomas Murphy, Miss Shaw. Here to see you."

"Ah." Josephine stood, and Tom would have missed the slight tremble in her hand if he hadn't been looking for signs of her temper. "Thank you, Mr. Carver. Would you see Mr. Burke out, please? He was just leaving."

"Of course."

Neville glared, but he didn't argue. He nodded toward his cousin. "Josephine, I wish you well."

"Of course you do."

Tom suppressed the smile at her sarcasm and held out a hand to the pale gentleman. "Mr. Neville Burke, I take it?"

The young Mr. Burke could hardly refuse his hand without it seeming awkward. He took it and Tom squeezed it firmly. Neville Burke looked like a man who'd spent his whole life in clubs and at dinner parties. His clothes were fashionable, his face soft. His pale blond excuse for a mustache hung limp beneath his narrow nose, as if it too had given up on any proper attempt at manliness.

Tom squeezed his hand a little harder to amuse himself.

"Mr. Thomas Murphy," Neville said through clenched teeth. "Your reputation, sir, proceeds you."

"I'm glad." He let go of the human's hand, resisting the urge to plant some mental manipulation that would banish him from Josephine's house forever. No, as offensive as Burke was, they needed to use him to understand what Beecham was up to.

"I understand," Tom said, "we have a mutual acquaintance. Mr. William Beecham."

Neville's face grew pale. "Ah. I mean yes, I am acquainted with the gentleman. You know Mr. Beecham?"

"Oh yes," Tom said. "I know all about Mr. Beecham. My brothers and I have known him for years."

"Is that so? How... remarkable."

Tom heard the waver in Neville's voice and noticed Josephine's eyes darting between the two men. This was taking too long. And Josephine was too bright not to pick up on the innuendo. He liked her intelligence, but he had to admit it was inconvenient at the moment.

"Good evening to you." He nodded to dismiss Neville Burke and turned his attention to Josephine. "Miss Shaw, I am honored to see your library." He bent and kissed her knuckles as the butler saw her cousin to the door. "My sister-in-law led me to believe it was extensive, and it does not disappoint."

"Thank you, Mr. Murphy!"

"It also gives me hope you will enjoy this gift."

He held out the slim volume to her and watched as she unwrapped it, meanwhile nodding politely at Mrs. Porter, who was knitting in the corner, and listening intently to make sure Neville Burke left the house.

Tom forgot the cousin entirely when Josephine's face lit. "*Ivanhoe!*"

"It is only the first volume, I'm afraid. I found it years ago at a bookshop in London. But the binding is good, and there's an intriguing inscription in the front I thought you might enjoy."

She held the book to her breast. "You brought me a

book."

"You seemed more the book sort than the flower sort. Though I'd be happy to get you those as well."

"A book." Her face was glowing. "You are quite adept at courting."

"No, I'm afraid I'm rather inexperienced in it. That's why I'm trying everything in the hope I'll hit on something that strikes your fancy."

She laughed then, and the butterflies took flight in her eyes. She opened the book and looked at the first page. "'To my own Rebecca,'" she read on the frontispiece. "Yours always, T." She looked up. "Your given name is Thomas."

"Aye, but I'm afraid I did not write the verse. Only acquired it with the book."

"Rebecca, not Rowena," she murmured. Her fingers traced over the script.

"Well," Tom said, "Rebecca was the more interesting of the two, wasn't she?"

"Yet Ivanhoe married Rowena at the end," Josephine said. "There's a story in this inscription, I think."

Tom shrugged. "Isn't there always?"

She held the book as if she'd found a treasure. "You're a *reader*, Mr. Murphy!"

If he could spend every night making her smile like that, proper manners and fancy dress might just be worth the trouble. "I am, Miss Shaw."

She motioned to two chairs by the fire, and Tom moved his seat a fraction closer to hers as they sat down.

"I would not have guessed," Josephine said. "Most of the gentlemen I've met since leaving school are not much for reading unless it is the newspapers."

A VERY PROPER MONSTER

"I can't claim to read philosophy or any kind of scholarly books. But I work nights mostly, so a good adventure story is always welcome to pass the time. *Ivanhoe* is one of my favorites."

"You work mostly at night? That's unusual, I think."

"I oversee most of our warehouses on the waterfront. Ships come in all hours of the day. Deliveries happen very early in the morning." *And the sun will burn me to a crisp.* "So yes, most of my hours are at night." He paused because the question was important. "Would that bother you? Should we...?"

She shook her head. "Not at all. I've always been a night bird. I sleep most afternoons and blame it on feeling ill." She glanced at Mrs. Porter, who only chuckled a little in the corner. "Mostly I just prefer the night. Sunlight can be quite harsh, don't you think?"

"I quite agree."

She started talking about books, a subject she was clearly passionate about. They talked about art and museums. About London and her favorite places and why she'd moved back to Dublin after school. Conversation didn't stop for two hours straight, even when Mrs. Porter started snoring in the corner.

Tom couldn't keep his eyes off her. She was delightful, as Anne had said. She was also intriguing, smart, and becoming more attractive every moment he spent in her presence. He was no longer merely resigned to marrying the woman; he was shocked to discover he truly desired it. And her.

"I wish you'd call me Tom," he said quietly, hoping not to wake her chaperone. "I know that's not very proper, is it?"

"Tom?" she asked, staring at him with wide eyes. "Only Tom? Not Thomas?"

"Just Tom."

She looked down for a moment before she looked up and met his eyes. "If I do, will you call me Josephine?"

"I don't think so." His heart kicked in his chest. "But I might call you Josie."

Her cheeks pinked. "Josie? No one calls me Josie."

"I do."

"Very well," she whispered, "Tom."

He took her hand in both of his. "Do you think... you might like to marry me, Josie?"

Josephine's smile lit up the room. "I believe I might."

Hello, butterfly.

CHAPTER FOUR

My dearest Lenore,

You'll think me caught up in one of my stories, but indeed, I am not. I am engaged to be married. His name is Mister Thomas Murphy of Dublin. He has two brothers, and he is old! But not too old. He is not handsome, but he is very tall. And, I daresay, his shoulders are dramatically broad. He does, as the housemaids have mentioned, cut a very striking figure.

We suit each other, Lenore. Far more than I ever expected a man to suit me.

I don't think we will have a large wedding. I don't want one, and I don't think Father will insist on it. Tom and I are both too old for foolishness.

I am happy and maybe a little frightened by it. It seems too easy. At some point a monster is sure to intrude, don't you think? We're going to the theater tonight. Tom (he insists I call him Tom) said we must celebrate because I did not cough once yesterday.

I like that he does not avoid my illness. He is

thoughtful but not overly solicitous.

I haven't told him about Miss Dioli or Mr. Doyle yet. It might be foolish, but I find I want to ensnare the poor man in matrimony before I announce my alter egos. (This will surely be my tragic downfall, don't you think? I can see the shadows lurking at the edge of this letter.)

He is no flattering suitor, which I like. He is, however, very excellent company and has a dry wit I value highly. He also gave me a copy of *Ivanhoe* with a very sentimental inscription. Do not reveal this to anyone (unless you're taken by villains and tortured for it, of course), but my intended might be a romantic.

Wish me luck, dearest Lenore. I have absolutely no idea what to do with him.

Your faithful friend,
Josephine Shaw

P.S. Tom calls me Josie. Isn't that grand?

JOSEPHINE held the handkerchief to her mouth, wishing she could shrink back into the seat. Wishing for the first time since she'd met him two months before that Tom Murphy would disappear.

"It was likely all that close air in the theater," Tom said, flipping open his watch and closing it. "I nearly passed out myself from Mrs. Lark's perfume. Horrid stuff."

Fidgeting. He was fidgeting. Tom didn't fidget.

"It's not too late to change your mind," she rasped out, then put the muslin to her mouth again to catch the cough. After the spell had passed, she continued. "It's not going to get better, Tom." Josephine looked up and almost reeled back at the anger on his face.

"Get your mind off that," he said. "What kind of man do you think I am?"

"A single man until next week. A healthy man. Not one who needs to be saddled with a—"

"Do not finish that sentence, Josephine Shaw, or you'll be insulting both of us."

She fell silent and watched the dark streets of Dublin pass, the steady trickling rain pattering on the roof of the carriage. Tom, never shy about ignoring propriety, shifted across the carriage to sit next to her. He closed his hand around hers, and she struggled not to pull it away.

"I want to marry you, Josie."

"Why?"

He was silent for a moment. "Well...," he finally drawled. "I'm quite eager to bed you, and you seem the kind who'll want matrimony for that."

Josie's eyes popped open and her jaw dropped. She swung her shocked gaze to his laughing one and tried pulling her hand away, but he only pulled it closer. "Tom!"

His eyes were all innocence, but the devil was lurking around his mouth. "What?"

"You did not just say that to me."

"I did. It's the truth."

Cough forgotten, her face felt as if it were on fire. "Mr. Murphy!"

"Is that what you're gonna call me when we f—"

She slapped a hand over his mouth. "Don't you dare."

He nipped at her fingers and pulled them away. He'd captured both her hands, and Josephine sat helpless, not sure whether she was more shocked or aroused.

Tom took a deep breath and smiled wickedly. "You knew I was lacking in manners when you agreed to marry me, Miss Shaw."

"What if Mrs. Porter were here?"

"Mrs. Porter isn't here. And I'd hardly talk about the pleasures of the marriage bed with my future wife while her companion was in attendance, now would I?"

Her heart raced. "Pleasures of the marriage bed?"

"Don't tell me you haven't thought of it. I know what kind of books you read."

"Tom—"

"Why are you embarrassed?"

Tom hadn't let go of her hands. He'd crossed them over his chest as if embracing her. Her fingertips flexed against the crisp cotton of his shirt, and she wondered at the thick muscle on his chest. He was solid as a wall. She couldn't even feel his heart beat, though her own was racing. His eyes were intent and his smile was still wicked.

"Come now, Josie. Why are you embarrassed? You're no blushing miss. Are you frightened?"

"I don't want to say." Her voice sounded tiny to her ears. She cleared her throat and tried to take a deep breath, but it rasped out of her.

Tom immediately let one of her hands go and put a cool palm on the side of her neck. "Shhh," he murmured.

"Easy now. I'm sorry. I was just teasing you. Try to relax."

"Hard to do with you so close."

He leaned away, but she grabbed his sleeve and pulled.

"Josie, I'm trying to—"

"I *am* afraid."

They both fell silent, and the only sound was the rain on the roof. She felt her face flush with embarrassment again. She closed her eyes and pressed her lips together when Tom's thumb stroked her neck.

"Why are you afraid?" he asked, his voice as hoarse as hers. "Is it me? I know I'm not—"

"*No*. Just... the unknown, I suppose. Reading isn't doing, is it?"

"No, it's not."

"And I can assume you have...?"

"Yes."

"Probably a good thing one of us knows what goes where then."

His chest rumbled with laughter, but his voice was gentle. "Josephine, open your eyes."

"Is my face still very, very red?"

"Yes, but it's lovely."

"Oooh," she groaned and let her head fall forward, only to feel his shoulder catch it. She pressed her face into his coat. "I'm very glad Mrs. Porter is not here."

"So am I." His lips touched her forehead. "Josie?"

"I'm going to hide here until we reach my home. As my intended, it is your duty to let me use your shoulder this way."

The aforementioned shoulder shook with more

laughter. "What are you frightened by?"

"Are you truly forcing me to speak of this?"

"Yes."

"Fine." She sat up but kept her eyes closed. "I have been informed by several well-meaning but terror-inducing friends and household staff that things do... hurt quite a bit."

"Hmm."

"That's the only thing you're going to say? 'Hmm?'"

"Nothing much to say about men who don't know their way about pleasing a woman."

Josephine had no vocabulary to respond to that.

"I can assume you know the mechanics of the act?" he asked.

"I'm an educated woman. Obviously, yes. Also... I have read more than one book that mentioned it."

"You're going to keep your eyes closed the entire way home, aren't you?"

"Yes, I am."

Tom laughed. "Fine. But even though you're hiding, you have to tell me..." He leaned close enough that she could feel his breath on her neck. "Your books? Do they... excite you?"

His voice moved along her skin like a physical caress.

"Josephine?"

"You know they do."

"Aye, I can tell they do by that gorgeous color on your face. Your lips are flushed and swollen. Your breathing is faster. But do you know what, Josie?"

"You have no manners at all, Tom Murphy."

"I know. Don't change the subject." His finger trailed

along the curve of her ear. "Do you know what?"

She was going to burst out of her skin. "What?"

His lips were at her ear. "I'm better than your books."

And when the gasp left her lips, he captured them with his own. Tom's kiss burned through her. One hand cupped her jaw while the other hand stroked her neck. His mouth wasn't still or chaste. His hands lifted her face to his until the angle suited him. Then, he devoured her.

His tongue licked out at hers, darting to taste her as if she was a delicacy he wanted to sample. He captured her lower lip with his front teeth and bit softly. Then his lips seized hers again. She heard him groan.

The hand holding her jaw slid back, and his fingers dug into her hair. They caressed the nape of her neck, tugging at her hair as his mouth—wondrous mouth—continued to kiss her senseless. Josephine felt the dampness between her thighs. Felt her small breasts swell as they pressed against his chest. His lips left her mouth and traveled across her cheek, nibbled her earlobe, slipped down to her neck.

"Tom..." Her eyes still closed, she held him close. One hand gripped the lapel of his coat while the other pressed to the nape of his neck. She could feel the shorn hair at his collar, the rough texture of his skin. She must have been feverish, because his skin felt *so* cool. She sighed when she felt the bite of his teeth at her flesh. A tingling against her skin. Sharp and teasing.

Tom's hand was still tugging at her hair.

"What are you doing?" she asked as he licked and kissed her neck. She finally opened her eyes, only to have them roll back in pleasure.

"Want your hair down."

She blinked. "What?"

"Hair. Want it—"

"No!" She pulled away. "Tom, we're in a carriage."

Did he actually just growl?

"Do you know how long it takes to pin my hair up? If you take it down, everyone in Merrion Square will know what you've been doing."

He pulled back, his lips pressed together. His chest heaved as he attempted to control himself, and Josephine saw him not-at-all discreetly adjust his trousers. Her eyes widened before she swung her gaze to the window again.

"You're marrying me next week, and then I'll have it down," he muttered.

"I usually braid it when I sleep."

"Not when I'm sleeping with you."

Could her heart beat any faster? "Oh."

"You still frightened?"

"Possibly more than I was before."

For some reason this amused him, and he laughed. "No, you're not." He reached out and took her hand, sliding his fingers between hers in a suggestive way.

Josephine shivered.

"You're marrying me next week," he said again, his voice bordering on smug. "I'll bed you then, and Josie? You'll like it."

"MISS Shaw? Mrs. Murphy, that is. Josephine?"

Was that Tom? Something cold touched her chest. Her back. Cool pillows at her neck as someone pulled the damp ones away and replaced them.

"Her temperature is no longer rising, but it is still very high. I would recommend a cool bath for most fevers, but because of her lungs—"

"Just tell us what to do."

Not Tom. The doctor. Tom had that lovely, deep voice that made her belly tremble for mysterious and exciting reasons. His voice had sounded so lovely in the church. It had resonated through the stone chapel as he said his vows. He was always so serious...

She heard someone sigh. "She needs fresh air. Relaxation." It was the doctor again. "Get her out of the city if you can. The air right now is noxious. It's the worst place for her."

Josephine struggled to open her eyes. "Tom?" she whispered.

He grabbed her hand. She'd know those calluses anywhere. "Josie?"

"Not... Not the wedding night we planned," she said before her chest was racked by another cough.

"Hush, Miss Jo." Mrs. Porter was there. She propped her up and untied her shift at the neck.

"Louisa." She tried to protest, but the cough surged up and stopped her voice.

"Now, child, you're married. I'll send the others away. None but your own husband here. Nothing to be embarrassed about."

Nothing to be embarrassed about? Her wedding night had ended in a fever, wracking coughs, and a house call from the doctor. Thank God Mrs. Porter had come with her to her new home. Poor Tom would have had no idea what to do otherwise.

Josephine finally felt strong enough to open her eyes. The room was lit by lamplight and full of more people than she was accustomed to. She could see her wedding dress draped over the chair in the corner of the room. Her new brother-in-law and sister-in-law were speaking with the doctor, and Tom and Mrs. Porter knelt by her bed.

He held a cool cloth to her head as Mrs. Porter eased her back.

"Wait here," she said. "I'll clear the room and bring the onions."

Her fevered eyes shifted to Tom. "And thus begins the romance of marriage," she wheezed. "It all begins with onions." She reached out and tried to smooth away the groove between his eyebrows. "Careful now. You'll look an old man too soon, husband."

"The doctor said it was likely the stress of the wedding and all," Tom said. "We should a' just run away, Josie."

"It's not your fault I fainted walking out of the church."

"No, but it'll give the papers something to write about." He pressed her hand to his freshly shaved cheek. "The poor Shaw heiress overcome by the idea of her wedding night with the scandalous Murphy brother."

Her rasping laughs turned into coughs. She closed her eyes again and focused on relaxing her chest. In. Out.

"Have you ever felt," she wheezed out, "as if you were trying to breathe through water?"

"Jaysus," he swore. "Don't do this to me, sweet girl. Give me a little longer, eh?"

She blinked her eyes open and lifted a hand to the

corner of his eyes where the skin was creased with age and worry. "Your eyes are all red, Tom."

He blinked and looked away. "Must be all the smoke. And worrying about you."

"I told you..." She traced a fingertip around his stern mouth. "I'm not going to get better."

"And I told you I was marrying you. And I did, wife."

She smiled. "That's right. We're married."

"We are."

"I like you so much, Tom. Far... more than I could have imagined. So unfair—"

Another coughing fit took her, and Tom helped her sit up, rubbing her back and placing the cool cloth at the nape of her neck.

"Tell me what to do," he whispered. "Anything."

"There's nothing... The onions will help," she rasped when the cough had passed.

Mrs. Porter bustled in, a smelly poultice in her hands and a stern look on her face.

"Mr. Murphy, sir, I must insist you clear your brother and sister-in-law from the room. The less company the better for Miss Shaw. I'm in no danger of infection, you see. I had it as a child and recovered. But the rest of you could be at risk."

"I'll clear them out," he growled. "But then I'm coming back to sit with *Mrs. Murphy*, so don't you bar the door."

She pursed her lips. "As you like."

The door closed a few moments later, and Mrs. Porter opened up Josephine's gown, carefully placing the steaming poultice on her chest. It was so hot she felt as if her skin would peel off.

"Oh, the smell," she groaned. "What horrid thing did you add this time, Louisa?"

"Smells like clear breathing is what it smells like. And the Murphys' cook had garlic. She said it might help."

"Well, it certainly"—Josephine coughed some more—"smells vile enough to be medicinal."

Mrs. Porter sat silently for a few more moments while Josephine breathed in the onion fumes.

"I think I heard them mention the house in Bray."

"Bray would be nice," she wheezed. "Take... you and Tom."

"And his valet, of course. Young man by the name of Henry. Seems a nice boy, and Mr. Murphy said he was good driver too."

The house at Bray was hers. Father had put it in her name years before. Josephine found she liked the idea of sharing the simple house with Tom. They'd planned to travel to Wicklow for their honeymoon, but Bray would be far more relaxing.

She felt herself slipping to sleep as her breathing eased. "Tell Tom..."

"What, dear?"

"See him in my dreams."

Mrs. Porter brushed Josephine's hair back from her damp forehead. "Course you will, lovey. Rest now."

But when she dreamed, Josephine was steeped in nightmares. Tom was there, but his eyes were bloodred and his skin ice-cold. He took her in his arms and kissed her, but when she pulled away, her mouth was bleeding and a childish voice whispered:

Are you afraid to die?

A VERY PROPER MONSTER

THE next time she woke, Tom was carrying her. She took a breath and realized the horrid onions had done their job and her breathing had eased. She pressed her cheek into Tom's shoulder, amazed by his strength.

"You're not even breathing heavily," she murmured.

"Are you awake then?"

"Hmmm." She burrowed into his shoulder. "Are we in Bray already?"

"We've just arrived."

"How long did I sleep?"

"Your fever broke around noon today, Mrs. Porter said. We both slept until late afternoon, then I decided we'd better get started. You woke a little in the carriage, but not for long. No coughing."

"Oh good." She took another easy breath. Ah, the wondrous onions. Vile, but effective. "I feel like a damsel in a novel with you carrying me like this."

A laugh rumbled in his chest. "Just to the house."

"No, no," she murmured. "You must carry me up to the top of a tower and ravish me. Or perhaps carry me over a hill as we run from bandits."

"I'm afraid there will be no ravishing until your strength is back." His voice wore a smile. He almost sounded as if he was laughing. "What an imagination you have, Josie."

"You have no idea."

"Are you a good one for stories? I love a good story."

"You might say that."

She felt him jostle her feet a bit as he maneuvered her through the small entry hall. The sea air nipped her too-long nose, and she could still feel the edge of the fever, but she didn't care. She felt as romantic as a heroine in one of her Gothic tales.

Which, being Gothic, didn't bode well for her long-term health.

She started to laugh out loud.

"What's so funny?" Tom asked. "Am I too clumsy for you?"

"Not at all. It strikes me that I am the sick maiden who is going to an isolated country house with the mysterious man who swept her off her feet and threatened to ravage her. This would make an excellent novel."

"Do you think so?" Tom leaned down and played with her, snapping his teeth at the tip of her nose. "Never fear, Josie, my girl. If I'm a monster, I'm a proper sort of one."

"Oh dear," she sighed. "A proper sort of monster? How very disappointing."

CHAPTER FIVE

TOM WOKE FOR THE NIGHT, his face already turned toward the door where Henry was chattering on to himself about some letters that had arrived from Dublin. The lad must have heard him move because he turned and gave Tom a silent nod that everything was well as he continued the one-sided conversation designed to give the illusion that Tom had been awake for hours.

"No sir, Mr. Murphy. I got them off to the post today, but there was nothing yet to bring to you." The lad paused. "Yes, sir. I'll check in the morning. Would you like to prepare for dinner, sir?"

Tom cleared his throat and said, "Yes, Henry. Please ask Mrs. Murphy to join me for a drink if she's feeling up to it tonight."

"Yes, sir."

Stepping closer to the side of the bed where Henry had already laid out a set of evening clothes, the lad leaned down and said, "Nothing unusual today, sir."

"Has my wife slept at all?"

"Yes, sir. Believe she woke for breakfast, then was locked in her room awhile with something or other. Slept this afternoon."

"No coughing?"

"Not that I heard, sir."

"Thank you, Henry."

"Did you need help getting dressed, Mr. Murphy?"

Tom waved him away, and Henry slipped out of the room.

It was one thing to plan to marry a human and conceal his immortal nature; it was quite another thing to accomplish it. Especially while traveling. The house he'd intended to rent in Wicklow was owned by immortals and had a staff who was fully aware of their secrets. But when Josie's doctor had suggested the seaside, he and Anne had quickly cobbled together a plan for Bray.

For the hundredth time since they'd arrived, Tom thanked the gods for Henry Flynn. The boy had been born to a couple who'd worked for Tom almost as long as he'd been a vampire. The lad had known about immortals since he was a child. Had never been terrified and had always known what it was to keep secrets.

Tom supposed every vampire had families like the Flynns. Or they did if they were lucky.

He kept his own chamber in Bray, which fortunately had very heavy drapes. And while he normally lay solitary in his secure day-chamber in his Dublin house, in the Bray house, Henry needed access to his rooms to maintain the illusion of humanity. The boy was trustworthy. That didn't mean Tom didn't help his loyalty along with a touch of amnis at times.

He'd planted subtle suggestions not to question his odd sleeping patterns in all the household staff and, unfortunately, his new wife. He hated doing anything to touch her mind, but it was necessary. Josie was simply too intelligent to fool by human means.

And gods, she was so very human.

Tom thought he'd planned for everything. But he could never have prepared himself for the feeling of helplessness that struck him when Josie was having one of her coughing fits. Or the raw guilt when he was forced to leave her at daybreak instead of staying at her bedside.

Tom wasn't used to feeling helpless. His relief at hearing she'd had another day with no breathing problems struck him as more profound than it should have been for a man who'd only met his wife two months before.

That made six days with no coughing since they'd come to the seaside. He'd promised himself to stay away from her for at least a week after her collapse following their wedding ceremony. Seven full days without coughing before he attempted more than a chaste kiss.

Oh, he'd have her, but Tom had to admit he'd been an insensitive fool. He'd not taken many lovers as an immortal. He found controlling his urges to be hard enough without adding in lust.

But Josie...

For once in his life, Tom had found a woman he enjoyed looking after. Maybe it was because she was so independent. Looking after her was a challenge. Her barely contained sensuality, a bonus. He still thought about their kiss in the carriage, though it did nothing to help his self-control.

His unexpected eagerness for matrimony and the anticipation of bedding his new wife had been all he'd been thinking of in the days leading up to the small church ceremony. She'd looked lovely in the church. In the back of Tom's mind, he'd imagined Josie dressed in a medieval costume with a flowing train and her hair falling past her waist rather than the fashionable dress and pinned hair she wore. That's what her dressing gown had reminded him of that first night in the garden. *No matter,* he'd thought. He'd have her hair down that very night and finally indulge his imagination.

But then came the horror of her collapse. The unexpected terror of her wracking coughs that simply *would not stop.* Tom had torn open her dress and corset in the carriage, which had helped, but it wasn't enough. Then her fever spiked. Then more coughing. Her father had tears in his eyes, terrified he was losing his daughter, though the sensible Mrs. Porter simply barked instructions at his staff as soon as she arrived, accustomed to her mistress's spells.

Tom finished tying his cravat, eager to see her again.

Six days. Tomorrow, perhaps.

Apparently his body still thought he was a boy of twenty, because even the thought of seeing Josie's hair fall down her back caused a very ungentlemanlike reaction. He straightened his waistcoat in the mirror and left his room, nodding to the maid as she passed him in the hall, noting her downcast eyes and ghost of a curtsy.

He truly hated acting the gentleman.

Following the sweet sound of Josie's voice, he headed toward the library where they usually enjoyed a drink before dinner. His wife was sitting by the fire, a book on her lap, interrogating poor Henry about his education.

"But you never went to school? Not even for a few

years?"

"Not... exactly, Mrs. Murphy. See, Mr. Patrick Murphy always kept... Well, see, there was—"

"Tutors," Tom said, rescuing Henry from the relentless curiosity of his wife. "My brother kept a tutor employed for all the servants' children. There were enough to justify it, and that way the girls could take the same lessons as the boys, which Anne insists on." He leaned down and pressed a kiss to Josephine's cool cheek, happy to smell less sickness and more of the gardenia-scented soap she preferred. "Good evening, wife."

"Good evening." Josie turned her head slightly, avoiding his gaze and the kiss he usually pressed to the corner of her mouth. "That's very generous of him. It's not many gentlemen who would keep tutors for their household staff."

Tom straightened, feeling the slight turn as if she'd given him a physical push. "Henry, if you would excuse us."

"Yes, sir."

The lad fled the room, and Tom stood next to her. "Tell me what's wrong."

A flush in her cheeks. "Nothing, Tom. You'll be happy to know I'm feeling well tonight. No coughing at all today. Did you accomplish everything you needed to for work?"

"Did I anger you? I did tell you I'd need to see to—"

"It's fine." Her pulse was rushing, and her flush grew. "I had... matters to attend to this morning as well. Cook found some lovely fish at the market today. I hope you'll enjoy—"

"Don't ignore me, Josephine. Tell me what I've done that made you turn away from me just now."

Her face reddened more, the flush spreading down her throat and across the high-necked dress...

One of her old dresses. Not one of the more fashionable evening dresses she'd ordered for their honeymoon like she'd worn the night before.

They'd played chess and he'd beaten her. Badly. Josie claimed she had no head for the game, but mostly she'd been making Tom laugh too hard with her stories as she narrated a melodramatic—and ultimately doomed —romance between the black queen and the white knight. It had him laughing so hard he could barely think to make a move.

They'd been laughing. Then he'd lost patience with her silly commentary and swung her onto his lap, kissing her soundly before...

He'd given her a chaste kiss and sent her to her bed because his own body was raging.

And tonight she was wearing one of her old dresses, and all the teasing light had gone out of her eyes because she'd mistaken his self-control for disinterest.

"Blast it, Josie!" He fell to his knees beside her. "No, no, no. It isn't you. I'm only worried—"

"It's fine." She turned her face to the fire. "I'm being silly. And... dramatic. It's a failing of mine. I know my spell after the wedding put everything in perspective. We're friends, Tom. I don't want to damage that. I value your company too much—"

"Friends?" He leaned forward, caging her on the blue chair though she still wouldn't turn her eyes to him. "You think I no longer want you as my wife?"

"Of course not. I know you'll make an excellent husband—"

"I'm not such an excellent husband if I've been ignoring what you need, am I?"

She shook her head, still staring at the fire. "I won't... I don't want to be a duty or an obligation. I have my pride. I'd rather have friendship than pity."

"Bloody hell." He grabbed her chin and forced her face to him. "You think my kisses are pity, do you? You think I don't want you? That I don't have to think of cold baths and the like when I leave you at night? I thought you were *dying* ten days ago, Josephine."

Her mouth trembled, and he saw the tears in her great dark eyes, though she blinked them back.

"I *am* dying, Tom." She put a hand on his jaw when he clenched it. "And I understand—"

He cut her off with an angry kiss. How dare she! Tom grabbed the back of her neck and pressed her mouth to his, swallowing the quick cry she let out before her hands came to rest on his chest and her slim fingers dug into the muscle there. She kissed him back, opening her mouth to his, and he tasted the sherry she'd been drinking. A hint of pear and a bite of something salty on her tongue.

"You understand nothing." Tom hissed before he kissed her again. He wasn't careful or chaste. She thought he didn't want her, or wanted her only for pity.

How dare she? How dare she make him laugh so? Make him hunger for her as he did? How dare she be so clever and generous?

So terribly mortal.

He pulled away from her mouth and bent to her ear,

biting the lobe before he soothed the sting with his tongue. He pressed his forehead to her warm temple and fought to control the drop of his fangs when he heard the swift beat of her heart.

"I *want* you," he whispered. "I want to see you naked in the firelight. I want to see your hair loose when you're wearing nothing but your skin. Want to see it brush the top of your arse. I want to see it tickle the tips of your pretty tits, Josie. I want my mouth on every inch of you. Want to feel you around me. Hot and—"

Josie slammed a hand over his mouth. "I don't want supper," she gasped. "Take me to my room."

Had he shocked her? Offended her? Tom swore. "Jo —"

"Take me to my room, Tom, and if you leave me without doing everything you just said, I'll... do something horrible to you. I don't know what. I can't think right now. But I have a good imagination."

He picked her up without another word and carried her out of the library, almost running over Henry on the way toward the stairs.

"Henry, tell Cook we don't need supper."

The lad's cheeks turned red, and he muttered, "Perhaps a tray later, sir."

"See that we're not disturbed."

"Yes, sir, Mr. Murphy." He nodded. "Mrs. Murphy."

Josie, seemingly oblivious to the interchange, had her lips against his neck. Her skin was burning, but it was the healthy flush of arousal, not sickness. He carried her to her bedchamber on the second floor. The evening maid was bending over the newly lit fire and jumped when he practically kicked in the door.

"Out."

"Yes, sir!"

She slammed the door on the way out, and Tom locked it behind her.

"We're shocking the servants," Josie whispered against his neck.

"If they're not scandalized by the time this night is over, then I'll consider it a personal failure."

He laid her on the bed and immediately set to undoing the buttons at her neck.

"I hate this dress," he muttered as he stripped it off. "Don't ever wear it again. Wear your new clothes. All the pretty things you bought. You should have pretty things."

"You can rip it if you'd like."

Leave it to the woman to make him laugh when his cock felt like it was going to revolt in his trousers if it wasn't released soon.

"Ripping corsets," he said as he unhooked her at the back, "is seldom as comfortable or as quick as novels make it out to be."

"Do you speak from personal experience?"

Her proper accent undid him. "You do ask the most inconvenient questions."

"I consider it part of my charm. Good God, you're right. Why are there so many layers?"

He finally removed everything but the thin cotton of her camisole. Her breasts pressed against it and he bent down, putting his mouth on them as she arched under his hands.

"Oh Tom!" she gasped. "That feels... I'm finding it very hard to describe at the moment."

Teasing his tongue over the thin cotton, Tom lifted

her and tried to remove all the skirts hindering him. "Much prefer the dressing gown," he muttered.

"What?"

"Nothing. Take everything off if you don't want it ripped." He started removing his own clothes, more than ready to join her.

"I thought you didn't believe in ripping clothes."

"I'm losing patience with ladies' fashions."

He stripped off the blasted waistcoat and shirt, ridding himself of the excess clothing before he turned back to the bed.

"Oh, I..." Her face was burning as she surveyed his bare chest. "Oh, my."

Josie lifted the edge of her camisole but didn't pull it off. Clad only in the light cotton of her undergarments, she was as bare as Tom had ever seen her. He decided to wait to take off his trousers. Best not to scare the woman.

She was nervous, which he supposed was natural. He climbed into bed next to her and pressed soothing kisses to her shoulder.

"We'll slow down," he said. "I'm losing my head like a randy lad, aren't I?"

She laughed nervously. "I lost my nerve when your shirt came off. You have a startling number of muscles."

And scars. And burns. His human life hadn't been an easy one. "I'm not so easy on the eyes as you, sweet girl."

"You?" Her eyes widened. "You're magnificent. Like one of those statues the Italians sculpt. And I'm so very thin."

He continued kissing her shoulder, teasing the edges of the lace camisole with his callused fingers. "You're good for my ego. I know I'm not a handsome gentleman.

And you're not thin. You're..." His fingers drifted between her breasts. "Slender. Gorgeous. Like one of the willow trees in your garden."

Her heart raced under his fingertips, but she said nothing. Tom's fangs throbbed in his mouth, but he beat back his instinct to bite. Tonight was about taking care of Josie. Bloodlust had no place here.

"Can I see you?" He reached up to tug at the pins he could see in her hair. "Here now, sit up."

She did, and he scooted her forward so he was sitting behind her. He leaned against the headboard, pleased at her shiver when he drew her back against his bare chest. "I've been dreaming about feeling all that hair against my skin. Let me take it down."

"If you thought the buttons were frustrating..."

He laughed and her small breasts shook with the movement. He grew impossibly harder, and he knew she felt it because her shoulders tensed.

"That does seem... rather impossible from my perspective. You realize that, don't you?"

"It's as natural as breathing. Just takes a bit of getting used to, like anything else."

"Are you abnormally large? Or are things always... proportional?"

Tom bit his lip to keep from laughing. "I think you're assuming a level of knowledge on a subject I haven't taken time to study."

"Oh?"

"And you're talking too much."

Her head fell to the side when he put his mouth there and tasted her. His left hand continued extracting the pins in her hair while his right cupped her breast

71

over her camisole. Slowly, he worked his hand under the fabric and finally, finally he felt her skin.

He groaned. "You're so soft."

"And you're not soft at all."

Her hair tumbled down, and Tom luxuriated in the chestnut silk that smelled of gardenias and lilac. Dark scents from her garden. Heady scents that wrapped around him as she arched back into his chest. He drew her hair around her as he eased the camisole off. Silk and warm skin and Josie. He banished the sickness from his memory and set his mind to her pleasure. He slowly turned his wife until her breasts were against his chest, and his hands trailed down her back, over the curve of her hips and the swell of her bottom.

"Let me," he said against her neck. He fought back the instinct to bite. "Let me—"

"Yes. Anything." Her voice was high and needy. "Everything, Tom."

Her trust undid him. He lay back, Josie draped across his chest, her hair falling around them like a curtain. His hands slid down, caressing the slick heat between her legs. He slowly worked her body until her eyes glazed over with longing and she fell to the side, begging for release. Then, with a gentle kiss, he pushed her over and she arched her back, shuddering with pleasure.

He carefully removed the rest of their clothes, scattering kisses over her skin and murmuring soft words to soothe her.

"So lovely, my wife." He lay at her side, his hands and lips arousing her again. "So perfect. So soft." He wasn't a small man, and he didn't want to hurt her, but some pain would be inevitable.

"Please," she whispered. "Don't make me wait."

Tom drew back. There were tears in her eyes and a tremulous smile on her lips.

"Josie?"

"I've waited so long," she said, her voice soft and urgent. "For you. For this. Don't make me wait, Tom."

He kissed her, pressing their lips together as he rose and parted her legs. He shifted up and felt the tight squeeze of her body. Slow. So slow. When her muscles tensed, he whispered and kissed her neck, pausing until her body melted for him again. He worked himself slowly to the hilt and then stopped.

"Josie?"

She nodded. "I'm... it hurts a little, but not as bad as I'd imagined."

"Well, you do have an awful imagination," he said with a smile, his body locked still so she could grow accustomed to him.

"You're not moving."

She squirmed beneath him, and he groaned.

"Wait for it. God, you feel good. Just want to give you a moment."

Josie reached up, stroking his cheek with her hand. "Oh, my Tom. You take such care with me."

She filled his heart and broke it all at once.

Tom couldn't hold back longer. He started to move. Josie's eyes fluttered closed, but her lips were flushed and red. Her heart raced, and he could feel the swell of her body around his, tight and slick. Her neck arched back, and he bent to kiss her again.

"I will never forget this," he whispered against her

lips. "Not a moment. If I live a thousand years, I will never forget this. Do you understand? I will *never* forget you."

She cried out and threw her arms around his shoulders, wrapping herself around him as he let himself go. Tom lost himself in her body, in the smell and taste and feel of her. Hunger for her blood forgotten, he fisted a hand around her wild tangle of hair and tugged, holding her in place as she writhed beneath him.

Josie. Josie. Josie.

She had captured him. Enchanted him. He'd never stood a chance.

He fell.

CHAPTER SIX

JOSIE'S CHEEKS ACHED from laughing as she walked into the library, Anne on her heels. The two had taken in a concert that had been advertised heavily for the previous month but had proved to be less than promised in person. They'd left early, and Josie had agreed to a drink with Anne before she slipped away to write.

"But the tenor—" Anne was laughing. "I think he might have been a she. I've never heard a man sing that high."

"It was extraordinary. Pity he was the only talented one among— Oh! Hello, Tom. What are you doing home?"

Tom was sitting near the fireplace... glowering.

Yes, she did believe that was the appropriate verb. To glower. Her normally composed husband was glowering.

Unsurprisingly, this did not make him any less attractive to her. Josie had become quite his sycophant, though she'd never tell him. In the three months they'd been married, her feelings had deepened to far more than mere affection for her rough-mannered, taciturn husband. She was, quite simply, besotted. And glowering did nothing to quash that.

"What are you doing back from the warehouse?" she asked, frowning.

Anne asked, "Is everything all right? I know there was supposed to be a meeting with Beecham tonight."

"And I forgot one of my reports. Realized I'd left it in Josie's sitting room last night, so I went looking for it." He held up an envelope. "What is this?"

"As I'm rather far away at the moment, I cannot tell you." Josie stepped forward with her hand out. "Give it here, Tom."

He flipped it away from her fingers.

"Tom!" She heard Anne slip from the room. "What on earth—"

"Who is Joseph Doyle?"

Her mouth dropped open. Her heart sped. "It isn't... I mean—"

"I can hear your heart racing from here. Tell me."

Josie frowned. "That's impossible. There's no way for you to hear—"

"Who is he, Josephine? Why is someone sending letters to a Joseph Doyle care of you at your father's house? Who is he? Is that why you've been spending your days over there?"

"You're mad." She'd raced past embarrassed and straight into furious. "I'm at my father's house every day because my father is *dying* and you're locked in your rooms working all the time! So don't question my—"

"Who is he?"

"He's me!" Angry tears pricked her eyes. She didn't know how to fight with Tom. He'd always been too kind. He was gentle with her, sometimes to frustration. A model of quiet humor and utter patience, even when she was at her most distracted. He'd never once raised his voice.

Glowering had turned to confusion. "What do you mean, he's you?" He frowned at the letter again. "Did someone mistake your—"

"Joseph Doyle is... a writer of... of Gothic stories and mysteries. He... That is, he writes for several of the more... popular papers in... in London. And he is... me." Her face was burning. She stared at the red and blue whorls of the rug at her feet. "Joseph Doyle is one of my noms de plume." She finally tipped her chin up. "I am sorry I concealed this from you, but I am not sorry I write such stories, nor do I have any plans to stop."

He was frowning at the letter, flipping it over in his hands. He stared at it, then cocked his head. Then looked up, a grin slashed across his scarred face. "Are you saying you write penny dreadfuls?"

She put her hands on her hips. "There are many fine writers in the Gothic genre who write for papers that—"

He cut her off with a clap of his hand on his thigh. "That's why you write so many letters. They're not letters; they're stories." He stood and started pacing. "Joseph Doyle sounds—" He snapped his fingers. "Did you write the one about the doctor who was murdering the old women?"

Josie stood frozen, blinking her eyes rapidly as Tom walked to her. "Did I write the... The one with the scalpel or the one who used poison?"

"Scalpel."

"No, I wrote the poisoner. Only it wasn't the doctor in the end. He was framed. It was—"

"The kitchen maid!"

Josie slapped a hand over her mouth.

Tom burst into laughter. "There's a lad on the docks who brings them from London every month. You have the most horrid imagination! The way you described those murders had my stomach churning, Josie. The jerking and frothing at the mouth—"

"And you *read* it?"

He was still laughing. He pulled her hand away from her flushed face and put the letter in it. "One of your noms de plume? Do you have more names I don't know about?"

"Viviana Dioli," she murmured. Surely she would wake up any moment to find that Tom disapproved of his wife pursuing such... unladylike hobbies. Not that she would stop, but she'd been braced for disapproval. Had her arguments planned in advance. But he—

"Viviana Dioli?" he asked. "Something tells me she doesn't write horror stories."

"Gothic tales of a more romantic nature."

His grin turned wicked. "I bet those stories have been getting a bit more detailed over the past few months, eh?"

Her face burned. Well, obviously.

"Any others I need to know about, Josie?"

"No, just... Are you telling me you don't mind that I write scandalous stories for London newspapers?"

He leaned closer. "Is it more fun if I disapprove?" He reached back and pinched the back of her thigh. "I knew that naughty imagination couldn't be just from reading books."

"No, it's been years of wicked mental cultivation."

She batted his hand away. "Are you laughing at me?"

"No." He smacked a kiss on her lips. "I'm relieved."

A spark of anger flared to life. "Did you really think I was having some kind of affair?"

"No!" He paused. "Perhaps. There's no way to answer that question correctly. To be fair, you were hiding things from me."

"I was hiding my hobby! Not a lover. And are you implying you don't have any secrets? *You*?"

He grew instantly silent. "Josie—"

"No." She turned toward the fire. "I'm still angry. Glad, yes, that you're not bothered by my writing, but also angry you assumed I'd do something so horrible. I would never be unfaithful to you, Tom."

She could feel him at her back. He carefully put his arms around her and rested his chin on top of her head.

"Forgive me, sweet girl? Jealousy isn't something I'm used to."

"I was a spinster for twenty-eight years. I hardly think—"

"You're clever and funny," he said, cutting her off. "You're generous and kind and beautiful."

"You're the only one who's ever thought so."

His arms tightened around her, and she ignored the tickle in her chest. Pushed back the threat of a cough.

"'Girls are caterpillars,'" he whispered, "'when they live in the world, to be finally butterflies when the summer comes.'"

She tried to turn, but he had her locked in place. "Where did you—"

"I see the butterfly you've become. And so do others. I don't like having to share you with the world."

Had he read *Carmilla* too? Or…

I saw no folly tonight. Only perhaps a bit of fancy.

That low voice in the garden months ago was utterly familiar now that she'd heard it in the bedroom.

"It was you," she said. "In the garden that night. You were the one I talked to."

"You were beautiful in the moonlight. Are you angry with me?"

"You saw me in my dressing gown."

The arms around her shoulders tightened, and she felt the laughter in his chest.

"I suppose… I'm not angry," she said. "Not about that. I wasn't angry when I thought it was one of our neighbor's servants, so why should I be angry it was you? Why did you—?"

"I was curious about you. I certainly never expected you'd be out in the garden in the middle of the night. I just wanted to see your home. And then I saw you, and I thought you looked like a fairy queen. In your white gown with your hair falling down your back. You had no fear."

"Oh no," Josie said. She managed to turn in his arms and lay her head on his chest. "I was wrapped in fear. I still am some nights."

Tom kissed the top of her head. "I don't ever want you to fear again. And don't hide anything from me. I want all of you."

"Then you can have it." *For as long as we have.*

AFTER they returned from Bray, Josie and Tom never spoke of her illness. While Tom had never shied from it before their marriage, something about them had shifted after those quiet, gentle nights of lovemaking by the seaside. Perhaps they were both living in a state of denial. Her breathing had been marginally better since their return to town, and she avoided any situation or event that could trigger an episode. She spent most nights writing or making love to Tom, who seemed to have an endless, fervent hunger for her.

He was her favorite form of madness.

They explored everything. After her initial nerves had been conquered, she found in her new husband an eager teacher. No question was unanswered. Often, demonstrations were required. They laughed when they loved, and Josie knew she'd fallen in love with Tom quite thoroughly, though she hesitated to say it.

There was a restlessness in her husband, and she knew, however he might accuse her of keeping secrets from him, his own secrets were a weight between them. There was a darkness in him. Too often, a sense of foreboding enveloped her. And her thoughts were... muddled. There was something she knew she wasn't seeing. She sensed he was a breath away from confessing something too many times to count. But the confession never came, and she didn't want to press him.

She didn't want to know.

She wanted to love. To revel in him. To gorge herself on life for as long as she had.

The heaviness in her lungs told her she didn't have long.

TOM and Murphy had announced the dinner party

three nights before, and Josie had found herself curious to meet some of Tom's business associates. The name of William Beecham was certainly one she'd heard in passing between Tom, Murphy, and their younger brother, Declan, but not with any great humor. She was surprised to find him invited to dinner. Even more surprised her cousin, Neville, would also be present.

"Has Neville tried to call on your father again?" Tom asked, straightening his suit in the mirror in his room before they descended to the drawing room. Because he worked mostly at night, he insisted on keeping separate bedrooms. If she were healthier, Josie would have objected, for she hated waking in the mornings without him. But for their situation, it made sense.

"Not that anyone has said. The servants would have told me."

"Any change today?"

She shook her head.

Tom feathered a caress across her cheek before he bent to kiss it. "He had a good life, sweet girl. And he's not in any pain."

"I know." She blinked back tears. "It doesn't make it any easier."

"No, it doesn't."

He turned to her with his cravat in hand and waited for her to tie it for him. It was a task she enjoyed and one he loathed.

"You know," she said as she tied the simple knot he preferred, "I never thought I'd do this."

"Tie a cravat? I agree. Wouldn't suit you."

"You know what I mean." Josie smoothed a hand down the front of his crisp white shirt. "I enjoy these wifely things. They're like... little gifts I never expected."

Tom caught her hand and held it silently. He opened his mouth, then closed it. He pressed a kiss to her knuckles and held her hand there.

"Tom?"

"I don't suppose those fantastic creatures you write of are real, are they?"

Josie laughed. "Vampires and demons and monsters in the night? Thank God, no. We'd all be doomed, wouldn't we?"

"Aye, but it wouldn't be such a bad thing to live forever," he said, almost silently, "if you could hold on to the people you loved. It wouldn't be so bad then, would it?"

It was as close as he'd come to speaking of her failing health since they'd been married.

"Was I unfair to you?" she asked. "Should I have refused this?"

"Never." He tipped her face up to his, and she could see the odd redness in his eyes again. Or perhaps it was only the light. "I'd not trade a moment of our time together, Josephine Shaw."

"Even when I'm acting like a madwoman when a story strikes me?"

"Especially then."

She choked back the lump in her throat and patted his chest. "You are the most patient of husbands, Thomas Murphy. We should go down before our guests arrive."

"Hang our guests. Murphy's the one who invited them."

"But I should not neglect my cousin. Even if I do find

him somewhat loathsome."

Tom grunted and held the door for her. "Why did we agree to host this?"

"Because Neville technically belongs to me. And our cook is better than your brother's."

"Don't say that. I might fire her if her food invites company." He kissed her neck. "Shall we?"

Though they were separate houses, Tom and Murphy's town houses near Mountjoy Square were adjoining and even connected through the lower floors. It was, in essence, one very large household, which suited Josie to the ground and allowed her and Anne to share much of the domestic burden.

Josie had been tickled to learn her night-loving tendencies were entirely indulged in Tom's household. Indeed, as her sister-in-law was usually busy during the days, Josie spent most of her time writing, which left the evenings free for family.

As they descended to the drawing room, she heard Anne's tinkling laughter rising above her cousin's nasal voice. As Neville had never been particularly amusing, Josie had to guess Anne was humoring him. Tom ushered her in, and she immediately caught the slightly pained look on her sister-in-law's face.

"You're finally here," Anne said. "Did Tom 'accidentally' lose his dinner jacket again?"

"Have no idea what you're talking about," her husband grumbled, kissing his sister-in-law on the cheek.

"Neville," Josie said. "How good of you to come."

Her cousin looked irritated that he'd been distracted from the lovely Anne Murphy.

"Hello, cousin. And belated felicitations on your union."

"Thank you."

Murphy came over accompanied by a pale gentleman with a rather unexpected halo of blond curls and a narrow nose.

"My dear Josephine," her brother-in-law said, "may I introduce Mr. William Beecham?"

"Of course," Josie said, inclining her head. "Mr. Beecham, welcome to our home. And thank you for joining us for dinner."

Cunning green eyes glinted at her before he bowed. His skin was frightfully pale, and Josie wondered at the temperature outside. They'd been having a mild winter, but Dublin weather could be unpredictable.

"I thank you for your hospitality, madam," Beecham said. "And my felicitations on your union as well. Seems Tom fooled you after all."

There was a meanness in his voice that made Josie want to curl into her husband. Perversely, that fear compelled her to be as clever as possible.

"I assure you," Josie said, tucking her hand in the crook of Tom's elbow, "any subterfuge was on my part. I hid all my most irritating qualities and hurried him to the altar. Poor Mr. Murphy never stood a chance."

The company laughed, but Mr. Beecham's gaze never left hers. They rested on her with a kind of furtive glee. As if he knew a secret she would soon discover and hate.

"Mr. Beecham, you must be a villain," she quipped.

Neville laughed, unaware the rest of the room had gone silent. "Why must he be a villain, cousin?" He nudged Beecham's shoulder. "Josephine tells the most amusing stories, William. She has since she was a child."

"Has she?" The handsome man's eyes hadn't left her. "Pray tell, Mrs. Murphy, why must I be a villain?"

"Your face is too handsome, sir, and your hair too angelic." She smiled innocently. "I daresay it is your fate to be a villain or a saint. And isn't a villain the more interesting role?"

Beecham threw his head back and laughed. "Tom, your wife amuses me. I quite approve."

She felt her husband tense when Beecham said he "approved," but he only said, "Thank you, Mr. Beecham."

It was the oddest dinner party Josie had ever attended.

Mr. Beecham clearly occupied some role of authority among the gentlemen, though he was vague about his occupation. Neville seemed to worship the man. Murphy and Tom offered him grudging respect, and Anne ignored him as much as possible. It was so unlike her husband to condescend to a man of Beecham's character that Josie thought she must have frowned at Tom through dessert.

She and Anne were the only ladies in attendance, so when the gentlemen called for the port and cigars, they both retired for the night. Anne, she could tell, had something troubling her. And though she was growing closer to her new sister-in-law, she did not yet consider herself a confidante.

She went to her sitting room, which doubled as her study, and started to work on the next chapter of the new story she'd been sending to Lenore. It was a departure for her, inspired by some of the fantastical tales of Jules Verne she'd been recently engrossed in. Her new husband was a fan of the scientific adventures, and she'd taken a liking to them as well. She was so engrossed in the tale of airships, resurrectionists, and questionably honorable demons that she missed Tom's entrance entirely. She looked up when the coals shifted in the fireplace, and he was sitting across from her, watching her work.

"Tom! I didn't see you there. Is it very late?" Josie struggled to focus. She was still lost in the story and wanted to finish the scene.

"Not so late," he said quietly. "Why don't I go change out of this jacket? I was smoking."

And smoke bothered her lungs, so he would change. Because he was Tom.

"Thank you, darling. Just give me a few more minutes. The heroine..." She drifted off, still thick in the middle of describing a haunting scene in a foggy graveyard. She was considering a new villain for the story. One with a high forehead, a halo of curls, and unnatural, glowing green eyes. After all, it was the most beautiful faces that hid the most horrible demons.

The fire was dying by the time she put her pen down. Tom was watching her again, stripped down to his trousers and shirtsleeves, lounging on the couch across from her desk.

"I love watching you work," he said quietly. "You frown and scowl. Then smile and cry. Sometimes I see your mouth moving when you say their words. Every emotion is on your face as you write. Is it whatever the character is feeling?"

She tried not to be embarrassed. "I don't know. Probably. Do you want to read this chapter?"

Josie had found Tom to be quite the excellent editor. Talking over story ideas with him had become one of her favorite pastimes, though he often laughed at the outlandish plot devices the newspaper audiences seemed to love.

"Course I want to read it. Has she discovered the hero isn't what he seems?"

"Yes, but I'm thinking about adding a new villain. One with blond curls and green eyes."

Tom smiled, but only for a moment. "Not too obvious, all right?"

"Would he even know?"

"William Beecham is... resourceful. Dangerous. If you ever meet him in town, avoid him. If you can't avoid him, speak as little to him as possible. And don't be clever or interesting. You don't want Beecham interested in you. He's interested enough as it is."

Josie blinked. "Tom, I was joking, but you act as if he *is* a villain."

"He's powerful. And not to be crossed lightly."

"Is Neville safe?" A chill crept over her, despite the warm room. "Why was he in our house?"

"He wanted to meet my new wife. Murphy thought it would be a good idea."

"Why?"

"We must do business with the man. We... condescend when we must. For now."

"He said he 'approved' of us." She couldn't stop the shiver. Mrs. Porter would say someone had walked over her grave. "What an odd thing to say. Who is he to approve of us?"

"He's..." Tom's eyes burned. "It doesn't matter. He

didn't approve enough."

"What—"

"Forget William Beecham." He leaned forward, elbows on his knees. "Josie, if there were a way to... cure you. If there were a way to get better—even if you had to leave Dublin—would you want it?"

She could feel the color drain from her face. "What?"

"If there were a treatment—"

"Stop." Her voice grew hoarse. "There's nothing, Tom."

"But if there were—"

"Don't you think Father looked? Do you know how many years I spent being poked and prodded? I've inhaled the most horrendous concoctions you could imagine. We tried sanatoriums and hospitals. I went to Switzerland, for God's sake. Don't be cruel."

"I never want to hurt you." His eyes were red again. "But if there was a way—"

"Stop!" She stood, knocking over her inkwell in her haste. She must have stood too fast, because it seemed Tom was there before she could blink, righting the bottle and blotting the ink so it didn't spill over her manuscript.

"Careful," he murmured. "I'm only asking. Didn't mean to upset you."

"Of course I'd want it," she said. "Don't you think I'd do anything to stay with you? I... I love you, Tom. So much. But there's nothing." She cleared her throat and felt the beginning press of tightness in her chest. "So please don't give me some kind of false hope. It's not fair."

He said nothing more. Tom straightened her desk, laid aside her work for the evening, then took her to bed.

He spent hours making silent love to her. He didn't return her words, because he didn't have to. Josie knew her husband wasn't a talkative man. His touch. His kiss. Every caress was its own declaration.

But to die as lovers may—to die together, so that they may live together.

What foolish words she'd once found romantic. Her lover could not die! Tom had to live so he could remember. Because if he remembered she had lived and loved him, then Josie could find the courage to say good-bye.

Chapter Seven

TOM TAPPED A PEN on the table as Declan finished up the monthly financial report for Murphy.

"I'd say the boat works will be profitable within two years with this expansion. While merging our existing works with Shaw's will cost in the short term, it'll be worth the investment."

"And Beecham?" Murphy asked.

"We'll be bigger, not just in holdings but in name. He won't like it."

Tom gritted his teeth. Murphy's refusal to confront William Beecham had become a bone of contention between them. Once Beecham had flat out stated the Shaw heiress was not to be turned—even before Tom had brought it up with his sire—any interest in concession had flown out the window. He wanted Beecham gone. Wanted Murphy to take over. And he wasn't quite rational about it.

Murphy tapped a long finger on the papers in front of him. "Beecham is... problematic."

"Beecham's a monster," Tom muttered. "And you'd have the support of more than half the immortals in Dublin. You don't hear what I do among the workers."

"And you don't hear what Anne and I do among the

gentry," Murphy said. "It's not a simple thing, Tom. If I'm to avoid bloodshed, we must tread carefully."

"There'll be no avoiding bloodshed," Tom said. "That's not how these things work."

"I have no interest in ruling a city where half the immortal population has been slaughtered and the other half only follows me out of fear."

"Why not?" Tom asked. "It works. Vampires respect power."

"They also respect intelligence. A bloody coup is not what Dublin needs right now. Not with all the unrest in human politics and not when the city is finally beginning to prosper. It's simply not wise. Neither is turning humans who are notable in society."

It was the closest they'd ever come to speaking of it, though Tom knew his anger at his wife's failing health had not gone unnoticed by his sire.

Declan was completely silent, and Tom felt an irrational spike of anger toward his brother. If Declan had been the one to marry Josephine Shaw, Tom would barely have known her. He'd not feel this tearing pain at the thought of her loss. He'd not have tasted the joy of her devotion only to have human disease snatch it away.

"Tom," Murphy said softly, "you knew it would end this way. It was why I forbade you from revealing yourself. It has nothing to do with my trust, respect, or affection for Josephine."

Tom slammed his hand down and stood. He tried to keep his voice level, but he knew he failed.

"If it were Anne—"

"But it's not Anne. There is a reason I've never allowed myself to become emotionally attached to humans. Added to that, Beecham has flatly denied—"

"Fuck Beecham!" he yelled. "We dance politely around the monster as he runs this city into the ground. He doesn't care about the people, vampire or human. He'll drain it like a docklands whore, and don't think he hasn't been doing more of that too. Is that the kind of men we are? To give allegiance to a monster like him? He isn't as smart as you, isn't as cunning as you, and he doesn't have the loyalty you've built. So why aren't you challenging him, boss? Why?"

Murphy stood and Tom tried not to shrink from the censure on his sire's face. It was instinctual, this need to please him. But other loyalties now tore at him, and Tom didn't shrink away.

"Your wife is human, and she is ill. There are reasons we do not turn the sick, Tom Dargin. And prematurely confronting a rival can lead to disaster. I'll not upend my plans for sentiment."

Declan slammed into Tom's chest and pushed him back before he could reach Murphy with bared fangs.

"Tom, stop!" his brother yelled. "Dammit, man. Leave it!"

He punched Declan in the face, tossing the man halfway across the room before Murphy was on him. He gripped Tom by the neck and shoved him into the wall.

"What do you think you're doing, Dargin?" Murphy said, his fangs bloody from piercing his own lips. "Stop acting the fool."

"You'll kill 'er," he choked out.

"She was dead before you met her."

Tom shook his head and shoved Murphy away. He had to leave. If he stayed, he'd do something unforgivable.

He couldn't change her himself. He knew that much. Any love they had would be twisted by the bond between sire and child. Stories of lovers who'd been changed inevitably led to nothing but tragedy and usually the death of one or both vampires.

But Murphy could change her. Anne could. Even Declan. Vampires he thought of as family. And yet they watched her every night as she withered away. She was failing along with her father. Her breathing was shallower, the smell of sickness around her more pronounced. More, her spirit—the playful, passionate spirit he'd fallen in love with—was withering. The haunted love in her eyes was enough to drive him to madness.

The water in the air drew to his skin as he walked, attracted by the rush of his anger and pain.

She couldn't die. If his sire refused to change her, then they would leave Dublin. Once her father was gone, he could convince her. He could go to Mary Hamilton in the north. He knew Anne wasn't unsympathetic. She loved Josie too. Tom thought Hamilton might turn her if Tom pledged himself to her service. She'd love to steal one of Murphy's top men.

Loyalty between his sire and the woman he loved tore him in two, but he could finally admit the truth.

Tom no longer wanted to live an eternity without Josie at his side.

"MR. MURPHY?"

Tom tried not to cringe at the name. Much of his

household didn't know his real name. His own wife didn't even know it. And the way he was feeling toward his sire at the moment, the last thing he needed was a reminder his life was not his own.

He turned and met Josie's companion in the hall. "Yes, Mrs. Porter?"

"She's not been feeling well today. Are you home for the evening, sir?"

"I am."

"She might enjoy the company. She can't seem to focus on her writing. I think she may be running a slight fever."

"I'll find a book to read to her then. Is she in bed?"

Mrs. Porter shook her head. "She didn't want the bed. I've settled her on the chaise in her room. Make sure she stays propped up. It's easing her breathing."

"Any news on Mr. Shaw?"

Mrs. Porter smiled sadly. "Mr. Carver did send word this morning that he thought it would be a matter of days, if that. Mrs. Murphy was planning on spending the night there, but I held her off until tomorrow. I thought she could use another night of rest."

"I'll try to get her to sleep."

"Thank you, sir. She's had a poultice tonight, so her breathing is easier."

"Thank you, Mrs. Porter."

Mrs. Porter started down the hallway, then paused. Turning to him, she said, "No, sir, thank you. She's had more joy and life in the past six months than the whole of the past six years, I think. I know your family is... different, sir. I wouldn't say anything more. But thank you. Thank you for caring for her as you do."

She swept down the hall before he could respond. And Tom turned to his wife's bedroom with a heavier heart and a renewed sense of purpose.

Six months of living was not enough. Not for Josie. Not for him.

He stopped by the library to grab a copy of Verne's *Around the World in Eighty Days*, which they'd been reading on nights she couldn't seem to focus on her writing. Not even the new adventure story she'd started seemed to be able to hold her attention for long. And if she was feverish, her mind would wander.

"Josie?" he said, peeking into the room to see if she'd fallen asleep.

Her eyes blinked open. "Hello, darling. How are Patrick and Declan tonight? Everything all right with work? You're home early. Anne was by earlier. Did you know she has a sister in Belfast? Isn't that interesting?"

Tom wondered if Anne's thoughts were running parallel to his. "I did. She and Murphy don't get along well."

"So I heard. What a drama." Josie smiled wanly. "Perhaps I should write it into a story."

Tom saw the unhealthy flush on her cheeks. "I brought a book to read. I thought we'd get back to old Phileas, if you like."

She held up her old copy of *In a Glass Darkly*. "I've been getting lost in this old favorite again. Read for me?"

"Vampires again?"

Did she know on some level? She'd never questioned his odd schedule, though Tom continued to use a nudge of amnis sometimes when she started to question why they spent every night together and yet he was always gone in the daylight. He hated it. Hated the deception. But if she discovered it on her own...

"I keep coming back to it," she murmured. "Something... I don't know. Familiar stories are like old friends, aren't they? They're comforting." She held out the book. "Please? We'll come back to Phileas another night."

And so Tom sat at the foot of the chaise lounge and put Josie's slender legs on his lap, stroking her ankles as he read from the tale of the mysterious vampire girl and the proper young lady she seduced.

> *"Dearest, your little heart is wounded; think me not cruel because I obey the irresistible law of my strength and weakness; if your dear heart is wounded, my wild heart bleeds with yours. In the rapture of my enormous humiliation I live in your warm life, and you shall die—die, sweetly die—into mine. I cannot help it; as I draw near to you, you, in your turn, will draw near to others, and learn the rapture of that cruelty, which yet is love; so, for a while, seek to know no more of me and mine, but trust me with all your loving spirit."*

He watched her as she dozed and he read the familiar words. Abruptly, she sat up.

"Josie?"

"I'd love for it to be real," she rasped. "Wouldn't it be grand, Tom? Do you think it could be real?"

"What's real, love?"

"The vampires, of course. Carmilla and Laura."

He choked on his desire to reveal himself to her, and she continued, the fever now burning in her eyes.

"There is so much more to this life than we know, isn't there? It could be real. It could be. Fairies and shape-shifters. Airships and demon lovers. Why couldn't they be real, Tom? Why would we dream of them if they weren't real?"

She'd started to cry, and he put the book away, pulling her to his lap so that he could hold her. He put his cheek against her burning forehead.

"'You will think me cruel, very selfish, but love is always selfish...' Oh, Tom! She was right. I'm sorry. It's horrible, isn't it? This love. To love someone and know they cannot be yours. We only borrow each other for a time, don't we? I'm too cruel to you, darling. Please don't hate me. I couldn't bear it if you hated me."

He rocked her back and forth. "Josie, please—"

"He was Irish. Did you know he was Irish? Joseph Sheridan Le Fanu. What a wonderful name. Not like Josephine. Who wants to read a story from a Josephine?"

"I do. I love reading stories by Josephine." Her skin was burning.

"Why aren't there more vampire stories? I wish there were. I wish I could have known him. My mother met him. They were... friends. Perhaps it wasn't the footman after all. He only liked Poe. But who doesn't like Poe, after all?"

She was rambling, her fever overtaking her reason. Tom stood and walked to the bed, stripping her out of her robe and ringing for the maid to bring some ice. Murphy kept a basement of it for blood stores, and Tom was tempted to take her down and hold her in the frigid walls of the cool room. He knew it wouldn't help.

A VERY PROPER MONSTER

"Josie," he said again. "Please, love. Take a deep breath. Try to calm down."

The breath she took rattled in her chest and made Tom want to rip the sheets and punch his fist through the wall. He put more pillows behind her and stripped the heavy, feather-filled blanket that only seemed to make her cough worse. The maid came, along with Mrs. Porter, and they began to see to his wife.

His wife. The love of his life. Tom could smell it in the breath she coughed out.

His Josie was dying.

Tom turned away before the women could see the bloody tears that filled his eyes.

TOM received word the next evening that John Shaw had passed away in his sleep, but Josie wouldn't hear it. Her eyes were half-open, and her breathing labored. She hadn't woken since her rambles the night before. Tom had been forced to his day rest, raging in fear that his wife would slip away while he was dead to the world.

Her breathing seemed a little better when he woke, but her fever had not lessened. Mrs. Porter and Josie's day maid had banished the doctor after it was clear there was nothing he could do.

Tom sat in despair, knowing she would never be well enough to travel to Belfast. He would lose her. But then he could end things. After all, he'd lived over seventy-five years, mortal and immortal life combined. That was a good run, he thought.

And Murphy?

Murphy could go to hell.

Tom lay next to Josie in bed, dabbing at her mouth with blood-stained cloths when she coughed. He paid no attention when he heard the door open or when Mrs. Porter announced Murphy and Anne's presence. He refused to look at his sire. These hours were not for him. He would hold his woman as long as he could. And when the end came, he would follow. Loyalty to his sire be damned. After all his years of service, what had Murphy done but let the woman Tom loved die a painful death?

"Tom," Anne called him. "Tom Dargin, look at me."

He didn't.

"Go away." Tom didn't want to leave her side, even to throw them both out. "Her father's dead. She's dying. Leave me alone. You won't have to bother with me much longer."

Murphy's voice was stiff. "Tom, stop this madness."

"Go fuck yourself." He brushed her cheek. "Sorry, sweet girl. I know you don't like rough language."

Anne was there, clutching his shoulder. "Tom, please."

"Won't be the same. Nothing was the same from the night I met her. My butterfly girl. Only woman as ever saw the whole of me. Loved me, she did. It'll be fine, Annie. No need to ask your sister for that favor. I'll stay with my girl until she goes."

"Tom, you can't be serious." Murphy banged his cane on the ground. "I sent Mrs. Porter away so we could speak freely. Stop this. This isn't you."

Anne was crying. "Tommy, please. We can't do without you."

"And I can't do without her!" He pushed Anne away, baring his teeth at Murphy as he roared, "Get the fuck away from us, both of you!"

Josie started to cough, sitting up on her own, her eyes open and glassy with fever.

"Tom?" she gasped. "Tom, who's yelling? What's wrong?"

He turned, ignoring his irate sire. "It's fine. It's fine. Here, love." He tried to get her to drink something, but the water only sprayed over the bed when she coughed again.

Murphy said, "She's mortal. You knew this when you married her."

"She's my mate," he said, not caring if Josie questioned him. She was already falling back into delirium. "Anne, get him away before I kill him myself. He don't belong here. Leave me be."

"You cannot mean to meet the sun," Murphy said, stubbornly standing at the foot of her bed. "Tom, your life is more valuable—"

"My life is not my own," he growled. "And hasn't been since I agreed to join you in this one. I cannot save her without driving both of us mad, and you've made your choice. But I tell you, I can join her when she goes. That is *my* choice. And you don't have any say in that."

"I'll lock you up."

"You plan on doing that forever?"

That shut him up, and Tom was able to concentrate on Josie again. His poor girl. She sounded like half of what she was breathing was water, but it was the fever that scared him.

"You're determined to die with her?"

Tom stroked her damp hair off her forehead. "I'll be dead already when she's gone."

He paid no attention to whatever silent arguments his sire was having with Anne. He watched Josie, watched the rise and fall of her labored breathing. Watched the fine skin of her neck where her pulse beat faintly. She'd be admitted to heaven without a doubt. He wondered if he was clever enough to talk himself in.

"Love you," he whispered. "I didn't tell you when you could hear me because I'm a fool. Thanks for loving me so well, sweet girl. You were the best part of this life."

"And who will take responsibility if she's uncontrollable?" Murphy said behind him. "Tom? He'd never be able to do it. So I'd have to, and we'd kill each other."

"It may not be necessary. She's never been a cruel person."

"She's dying and feverish. You know why there are rules against—"

"I'll do it," Anne whispered. "I love her too, Patrick. Do this, and if she is mad—if she cannot be trusted—I will take responsibility for her. You know I can."

Silence fell. Then Tom felt the touch of Anne's hand on his shoulder.

"Tom?"

"Go away."

"Tom, step away from her. Let Murphy do what he needs to. You don't need to be here for this."

He lifted his head. "What are you talking about?"

"You're sure she would want this?" Murphy asked him, tearing off his jacket and rolling up his sleeves. "She never knew the truth of who you were. You're *sure*, Tom?"

He blinked, in a daze, unsure of what he was seeing.

"Positive. What are you doing?"

"What do you bloody think I'm doing?"

Anne pulled him away from Josie's bedside, and Murphy sat on the edge, brushing the hair from Josie's neck.

"Anne, find something to tie her hair back."

Tom stood gaping. "But Beecham—"

"I'm not losing my own bloody child because Beecham wants the Shaw family dead. Hang Beecham. We'll do this, and soon I'll be the lord of Dublin, but only if you're at my side. Do you understand me?"

"Yes, boss."

"She's dead to the world. Do you understand? She's not in society, mortal or immortal. She died this night. And she'll stay dead until everyone who remembers her in this life is gone. Can you live with that? Can she?"

Mad hope had finally pierced the shadow around his heart. "We'll make do. I'll take care of her. Always. I promise."

"Of course you bloody do. You're the most stubborn, loyal bastard I've ever met. Don't know why I fooled myself that you'd let her go." He tilted Josie's neck to the side. "Now tell the cook to start bleeding all the servants who haven't given in the past month and pray to God this works."

IT took Anne and Declan both to wrestle Tom out of the room, even though the big man knew it was necessary. The process of turning was not far from the process of death. Even now Anne and Declan would be spelling the few servants who didn't know of their true natures and sending them away, while the others gave blood before retreating to the safety of Murphy and Anne's house. Away from the danger. Away from the newborn who would wake.

Murphy had removed half the woman's blood when he heard Anne return. Josie's heartbeat was failing, so he drank faster. It tasted... wrong. He spit most of it into the basin beside the bed, not wanting to chance any kind of strange reaction. He'd never fed from anyone as sick as Josephine, and though he knew vampires were immune to human disease, some instinct told him too much of her blood would make him ill.

"Stop for a moment," Anne said.

He drew back and she wiped his mouth, bending down to take his mouth with hers. Then she brushed a hand over his cheek and gave him her wrist. "Take some of mine. You'll need extra since you're not taking much of hers."

"This is already so risky. I don't want to chance it."

"I agree."

He bent to Josephine's neck again. It was not such an easy thing to drain a human—especially when not in the throes of true bloodlust—but her blood had to be removed to the point of death before he gave her his own.

Minutes stretched as he held the poor thin woman in his arms, killing her to save her. Finally—when her heart began to falter—he put her mouth to his wrist.

"No," Anne said, pulling his collar down. "As much as I hate the idea, she needs to take your neck. Your wrist won't be fast enough."

"Are you sure?"

Anne was his mate, and as much as he loved Tom, his first loyalty was to her.

"And I can't do without her! She's my mate."

It was the pain of those words that finally convinced him, because Murphy knew Tom spoke the truth. Nothing he could do would save his dearest child if Josephine Shaw was allowed to die. No political maneuvering, no intricate plan, and no cultivated reputation would excuse Murphy in his son's eyes.

So Josephine must live.

Anne slashed his throat with her own fangs and held the girl to his neck, forcing the blood into her body. His mate held them both until Murphy felt the first stirrings of amnis in the girl, felt her own fangs lengthen and grow, latching on to his neck with vicious hunger. Amnis, the energy that would bind her to him as his immortal child, flowed over him and into her, resurrecting her, tying them for all time. She was his, but he was hers too. For as long as she lived, Murphy would be responsible for her. Care for her. With every child he sired, he gave up a small part of his soul.

He hushed her when the small groans of pain crept through. He smoothed her hair back and held her as her body began the process of turning. Anne stood on her other side, ready to help her friend's transition into immortal life.

Josephine Shaw would live. But she would never be the same.

CHAPTER EIGHT

SHE BOLTED UP IN BED, almost throwing herself into the fire with the unexpected strength of her limbs.

"Josie!"

She screamed when she hit the floor. And she kept screaming.

The hunger.

The pain.

She was in the throes of a most horrific dream.

Her throat burned. Her mouth ached. The room burned. There was a roaring in her ears and a tumult of voices surrounding her.

"Put out the fire, it's too hot!"

"Is the bath ready?"

"Josie? Josie, try to drink."

A goblet was forced to her mouth, thick with the scent of copper and meat. Blood. It was *blood*. She choked on it until the taste hit her tongue, and then she opened her throat, howling inside from the pleasure.

"Another. Give me another, damn you."

"Bath is ready, boss."

Her body hit the water, and it was hot and cold all at once. She tried to scramble away until she felt him at her back.

"Shhh." His voice captured her and she turned to it. She blinked her eyes open before she closed them again, wincing.

"Turn the lamps down. They're too bright. Josie? Josie, love, can you hear me?"

"She needs to drink more."

The water crawled up her body, and it was her friend. It petted her as if she were a cat curled by the fire. It was a cool blanket on a warm day. Her nurse's soft touch.

"Josie?" Another goblet shoved under her nose, and she grabbed it with both hands, feeling the metal bend under her fingers.

"What?" she croaked. "What—"

"It's all right now. Just drink."

"Tom?"

"Drink, Josie."

She drank. And then she drank some more.

Liquid heat. Satisfaction.

I'm dreaming. This is a dream.

"You're not dreaming, Josie."

I've died. I was so afraid to die. I left him. My lovely Tom. I left him.

"I'm here, sweet girl. You didn't leave me. You're right here."

She closed her eyes to block the light, weeping with the pain of losing him.

And when the tears touched her mouth, they tasted of blood.

HENRY Flynn put his arm around Mrs. Porter as he

showed the old woman into the room where Mrs. Murphy's body lay. He'd be grateful when all the new servants were gone and only the ones that knew the truth were left. He'd grown weary of the lies and constantly guarded words. His father had told him he'd be expected to do things like this, but he'd had no idea how complicated it would all be.

Lucky the missus was a vampire now. At least he'd no longer have to carry on one-sided conversations for hours while the master slept. But Mr. Tom Murphy was about as grand an employer as he'd ever have, so he wasn't about to complain. He was very grateful the man wouldn't have to say good-bye to his wife, who was now lying in the darkened room, the fire low and the covers drawn up to protect her as much as possible while they fabricated the story of her death.

According to his mam, she'd wake at nightfall with a driving hunger that wouldn't know friend from foe, so it was important that all the human visitors be ready to leave well before dusk.

"The poor girl." Mrs. Porter sniffed. "The poor family. Mr. Shaw gone and Miss Shaw too. All within a day. And poor Mr. Murphy."

"He's in his room now," Henry said. "He weren't in a good state last night."

"Well of course he wasn't," Mrs. Porter said. She put her arm around Mrs. Murphy's day maid. "They loved each other so. What a tragedy."

"It is," Henry said. "Though I know my master wouldn't have traded knowing her for anything."

"Oh, poor Mr. Murphy!" the maid said. "And poor Miss Shaw. It's so sad, and yet so terribly romantic, don't you think? Miss Shaw would have liked that."

"Here now," Henry said, trying not to shake his head at the maid's melodrama. "Why don't we go downstairs? There's nothing of her here. The downstairs maids will clean the room, and I know others will want to pay their respects. Let's go see if Cook has anything to eat, shall we?"

He ushered both the grieving women downstairs and into the care of Cook while he saw to the other men on the floor who were guarding the master and the missus. Hours passed as Henry began the business of faking a funeral. It shouldn't be too much trouble. His father had faked one for Mr. Declan. It'd be easier if he had a few more men, but currently, most of Mr. Murphy's staff were busy securing the day-chambers until the vampire staff rose at dusk.

Henry was hoping when they were both sorted he'd be able to consolidate security for the two of them. Guarding one day-chamber would be so much easier than—

"Unhand me!" A domineering voice rang from the ground floor.

"But Mr. Burke! Surely you can wait for tonight. Mr. Murphy is retired and he won't want to be dist—"

"I want to see my cousin! Take me to her now."

"I say, who do you think you are?" Adams, the old butler, had never been one to mince words. "Sir, Mr. Murphy is not receiving callers at this hour. You must leave."

Henry stood at the top of the steps while Mr. Neville Burke made a great show of trying to look like a worried man. Henry wasn't fooled. Burke had the gleam of greed in his eyes.

"Mr. Burke, sir," Henry interrupted his rant. "I'll ask that you don't step any further into the house."

He was in a precarious position. Henry was only a servant. As such, if Mr. Burke wanted to barge in, he'd be able to with neither of the Murphy brothers to stop him. The only people awake in the house were servants, and the last thing anyone needed was for a constable to be fetched if Mr. Neville Burke thought the servants were trying to keep him from his cousin.

"And who are you?" Burke asked.

"I'm Mr. Murphy's valet, sir."

"And where is your master, boy?"

"Grieving, sir. Mrs. Murphy died night before last."

"Oh no." Neville Burke did not look surprised. He climbed the stairs toward Henry. "My poor cousin. Take me to her. Let me pay my respects while I still can."

"Mr. Burke—"

Neville Burke grabbed him by the collar. "Take me to her."

Henry could see a stain of pink in the sky. Perhaps if he showed Mr. Burke the body, he would leave quickly. The longer it took to get him out of the house, the more dangerous things became.

"Of course, Mr. Burke."

He shook his head at the panicked face of the guards on the second floor as he escorted Neville Burke to the mistress's bedchamber. All the curtains had been drawn, and only the ghost of a fire had been lit. According to the master, she would wake after him, her younger vampire body needing more rest. Still, it wasn't as if Henry was at ease around her. He'd been told since he was a boy how dangerous it was to be in a room with a newborn vampire. He kept the door to the hallway open, ready to run.

"Oh, my sweet cousin."

Mr. Burke leaned over the bed, a bit *too* interested, by Henry's reckoning. He was holding a hand over Mrs. Murphy's face as if checking her breathing. She wouldn't be. Vampires didn't need to breathe unless they wanted to smell the air or speak.

"Now that you've paid your respects—"

"I'll sit, boy." He drew a chair to Mrs. Murphy's bedside. "I've heard some interesting rumors about my dear cousin's husband, and I'm keen to allay any suspicion he might be under."

Henry's heart began to race. "Mr. Burke, that isn't a wise idea."

"Why not?"

"Mr. Murphy... he wanted his solitude for sure. When he wakes—"

"Ah yes," Mr. Burke said. "It will be interesting to see what happens when *Mr. Murphy* wakes."

"I'm not sure interesting is the right word," Henry muttered.

"What was that?"

Henry took a deep breath and hoped Mr. Tom would be waking soon. It was usually as soon as the sun fell below the horizon.

"I'll just... watch the door, Mr. Burke."

"Good lad," Mr. Burke said. Then he sat back and waited.

Henry heard a thump down the hall and prayed it was Mr. Tom. If he would just get here...

"By God, she moved."

It was only a whisper.

Henry's heart pounded out of his chest. "A trick of the light, Mr. Burke. Come with me, please."

"No, it was no trick. My God, Beecham was right. There's some kind of black magic—"

"Mr. Burke!" Henry's voice was panicked. He'd seen the twitch. The mistress was waking early. "Come with me. Come with me now if you want to live."

"What is this sorcery?"

Henry could wait no longer. He ran to the bedside to grab Neville Burke, but by the time he reached him, Miss Josephine's eyes were open and staring at her cousin.

She glanced at Henry for only a second, and she whispered, "Run."

Henry ran.

JOSIE'S eyes took in everything. The dim light of the room was nothing to her. She saw every shadow flickering by the firelight and the unholy gleam in her cousin's eyes. She smelled him too. Onions and roast beef. The musk of his sweat and the pungent scent of oil and gunpowder. He smelled disgusting. And appetizing.

"Hello, Neville."

"What's wrong with your voice? What are you?"

The burning was still there, but not like she'd dreamed. She was Carmilla, stealthy and secret.

"I'm dreaming," she whispered, closing her eyes. "And I shall not wake again."

"Jo?"

She could hear it thrumming, his heart, like the beat

of a hummingbird's wings. It called her. Her neck arched back when she felt the fangs she'd dreamed grow long in her mouth.

"Josephine? What the bloody—"

She was silent when she leapt on him, knocking him off the chair and backward toward the fire. She reared away. No fire. Fire was bad.

"Josephine!"

He was starting to scream, and that wasn't good. She put a hand over his mouth as she dragged him away from the fire.

"Shhhh," she whispered. What a repulsive creature he was. He'd broken her dolls' faces when he was a child. Cut chunks out of her long hair. And look how weak he was! Josie was dragging Neville about the room as if he were her new doll.

He fumbled for something in his jacket, but Josie stopped and dropped him, transfixed by the dust motes dancing in the air. Everything moved as if underwater. Neville's voice was murky as he pulled something out of his pocket.

It was a gun. Pointed at her.

She laughed because she heard the thundering steps coming down the hall.

Silly Neville. What was he thinking to bring a gun into Tom's house?

"I'm warning you, demon. Release my cousin. You have no power over—"

The chamber door crashed in and the gun began to swing toward it.

"Demons!" he screamed. "Unholy monsters! He was right! William was right! I'll kill you all!"

"No," she whispered. What if her stupid cousin shot Tom? He wasn't allowed to do that.

Before she finished thinking it, she had knocked Neville to the ground and batted the gun away.

"No!" she screamed, and then the anger and heat and hunger took her. She pulled his neck up and clamped her mouth over the hammering pulse in his neck. Josie drank deep, shaking Neville when he shouted, batting at his head when he tried to squirm away. Her prey fell still, and she drank.

She fed until the pull of her hunger lessened, then she let Neville's body fall and sat back, still crouched over him when she caught the edge of her reflection in her dressing mirror. She cocked her head at the strange creature she saw.

A dark curtain of hair hung around her face. Her skin was pale, but luminous in a way she'd never noticed before. Strange green eyes went wide with delight at the curious creature in the mirror. Blood dripped down her chin, and her mouth hung open as the edge of sharp white fangs sparkled in the lamplight.

She reached up and touched them with wonder, then her eyes searched for Tom, who was standing motionless in the doorway wearing nothing but his trousers and a guarded expression. She smiled when she saw he had fangs too.

"Tom," she said, lifting a dainty, blood-covered hand. "Look at me. Aren't I the pretty monster?"

SHE couldn't stop touching him, but Tom didn't seem to object. He held her on his lap, though he'd ignored her wishes and donned a shirt. Josie kept pushing things and lifting them, enamored of her new strength.

"Tom?" she asked, lifting up her arm. "If I cut myself, will I bleed?"

"Yes. Don't cut yourself."

"I was just curious." She pushed his shoulder and felt it give. "I'm so strong now."

"I know you are." His voice was everything. It was love and relief and laughter. It was the most seductive thing she'd ever heard in her life. She was hungry for so much more than blood, but Tom said they had to wait for Murphy.

"Are you laughing at me?" She stroked the creases around his eyes. He was so handsome. Well, not to everyone, for his scars and wrinkles would never make him handsome to the fools of the world. But he was the most handsome man in existence to her.

"Maybe a little," he said softly. "I'm so happy. Are you happy? Are you content with this?"

"Tom, listen." She put a hand on his chest, then she took the deepest breath she could, letting it out slowly as she smiled. "Grand. I feel grand."

"So you're not too angry with me?" Tom asked. "For not telling you the whole of it?"

Josie laughed. "I wouldn't have believed you! Who would believe this? I'm not sure I truly believe it yet."

She turned when she heard the door. She tensed until she saw it was Anne and Murphy. Her eyes filled with tears and she stood, holding her arms out to Murphy. "I love you," she said. "So much. Both of you. Though mostly I love Tom."

Murphy embraced her, then Anne.

"We love you too," Anne said. "How are you feeling?"

"Hungry."

"How about me?" Declan came in behind Anne. "Do you love me?"

Tom made a noise and Josie turned back to him.

"Was that a growl?" she asked. "Did you really growl?"

"Maybe."

"Can we turn into great cats like in the book?" She tried not to bounce. "Is that why you can growl?"

"No. That's just a story."

Declan scoffed, "What books has she been reading?"

"You say it's just a story," Josie said. "But so were vampires until I became one. I'm a vampire..." She sank into the chair next to Tom. "How marvelous."

"Boss, what are we going to do about Burke?" Declan asked Murphy while Tom stayed suspiciously silent, guarded eyes pointed at his sire.

Josie tried to stir up some guilt about her cousin, but she couldn't seem to grab onto it properly. After all, Neville was odious. And he'd been about to shoot Tom.

"I'll tell Beecham the truth, of a sort. The human invaded my home and was about to shoot one of my people. He won't make a fuss. After all, it is evident from what Josie said that Beecham has been filling Burke's head with stories. He won't want that getting out, will he?"

"And Josie?"

"I told you, as far as the world is concerned, she's dead. Josephine Shaw Murphy died two nights ago, and you're going to bury her in a grave two nights hence."

Josie gasped. "May I go? I'd love to go to my own funeral."

The answer was a unanimous and choral "No."

"We're not telling Beecham then?" Declan said.

Murphy shook his head. "We can work this around to harm him. If I attack him now, we'll lose too many people. Aggression creates enemies. I don't need enemies, I need allies. In time, we'll let it slip that Beecham was the one who told Neville Burke about us, leading the man here. The more conservative vampires in the city will shun him. They'll start looking for a replacement."

Josie smiled. "And that replacement will be you, of course. Mr. Murphy, you are an excellent plotter. Well done!"

"Thank you, Josephine." Murphy smiled. "But I think you can call me Murphy now."

"ARE you sure?"

Tom was talking again while she tried to seduce him. How irritating.

"I'm sure," she said. "Kiss me."

They'd fled to the safety of Tom's bedchamber as soon as possible. He informed her they'd only be a few weeks in Dublin before he moved her someplace more secure with fewer humans and less temptation. He only needed to stay in Dublin long enough for her funeral and to appear properly grief stricken to anyone who might be watching.

Josie decided she wouldn't mind being farther away from people. Even now, she could smell the lingering scent of blood filling the hallways, though all the mortal servants had fled to Murphy and Anne's house next door. She wanted Tom to distract her. Also, she wanted to kiss him. As often as possible.

"I don't mind," she said again. "Kiss me."

She groaned in pleasure when he stripped off her clothes. The feel of them, like anything to do with her senses, was rough and angry on her nerves. The lights were all doused, but she saw without effort. The room was cool and comfortable. And Tom...

He was temptation incarnate.

It had been a nonstop flood of information since she'd woken that night. Well, there had been the violent episode at the beginning, but that was already far from her mind. Someday, when she could think of something other than her own hunger, she might take the memory of Neville out and feel guilty.

But of course, she reminded herself, he *had* been about to shoot Tom.

Oh, Tom.

Her husband clamped his mouth down on her neck, bracing himself between her thighs as he teased her body to violent arousal.

"I'm stronger," she gasped. "You won't have to be so careful anymore."

"I know." He nipped at her skin. "Josie, can I..."

"What? You can do anything you like, Tom. Always."

"Be careful offering gifts like that."

"What do you want?"

"To bite you." He captured her mouth and teased her fangs, which were deliciously sensitive.

"To drink? From me? Is that... done?"

"Yes. And then you'd bite me."

Oh, her body liked that idea very much.

"Oh, yes, please," she said, writhing under him. "Now, in fact. Please do that now."

"It's a blood tie. A bond between us."

"Silly man. Are you hesitating for me? We're married already."

He pulled back and looked into her eyes. "This is permanent, Josephine. Not anything that can be broken. Not even by the Church. If I take your blood and you take mine, we'll live in each other forever."

Josie stroked his cheek and smiled. "Like I said, silly man, we're already wed. I promised to love you till I die."

"You did die."

"No." She kissed him and scraped her fangs over the thick muscle of his neck. "I lived. And you are my life now. My very proper monster. I love you, Tom. Forever."

He kissed her as he took her, and Josie felt her soul slip free. She tilted her head back and bared her throat to him. His fangs pressed and sank in, claiming her on the most elemental level as he drove them both closer to release. She held on to him until he pulled back, then he bared his own throat to her, and she tasted her lover's blood, rich with the scent of sea and salt and whiskey. She was lost in him, and he in her.

Her husband.

Her hero.

Her Tom.

Chapter Nine

TOM WOKE THAT NIGHT with a dream in his arms. His Josie, safe. Strong. Healthy. She was a revelation. She was *alive*.

And far from resigned to her immortality. Josie seemed to rejoice in it. But then, if it was possible any human might be born to become a vampire, it would be his Josie. Her morbid imagination existing side by side with her humor and appreciation for life was unlike any other human he'd met. She reveled in the monstrous. She delighted in the macabre.

Keeping her away from her funeral was going to be a challenge.

Tom heard a knock at the door.

Leaving her in the bed they could now share, he walked silently to the sitting room. He smelled Anne on the other side of the hall door and cracked it open.

She held out several jars of fresh blood. "Fresh from the kitchens. Tomorrow she starts getting chilled. We've gone through the available staff."

"Fair enough."

He waited, wanting to close the door but sensing she had more to say.

"He wasn't being cruel, Tom."

"So you say."

"He loves you."

"And I love her."

She waited, lips pursed. "I know that. But he didn't. Not till the end. Would you have done it? Would you have met the day if she'd died?"

He tilted his chin up, displaying the marks he'd not allowed her to heal. Her own claim on him, as she bore the scars from his first bite.

Anne nodded. "I see. She truly is your mate then."

"It wasn't a bluff. I don't bluff. She's it for me, Annie. Was from the moment I saw her, I think."

Anne glanced over his shoulder. "It's early yet. There's no way of knowing how she'll adapt. She could be mad, Tom."

"She won't be." Tom was sure of it. A bit off at times? Maybe. But she had been in life too. Her genius was its own kind of madness, but her kindness had survived her death. "It's no matter to me. I'll love her anyway. Keep her safe. I promised to care for her as long as we live. I never made that kind of promise before her, and I don't plan on breaking it."

Lifting to her toes, she kissed his scarred cheek. "You're a good man, Tom Dargin."

"Maybe." He shrugged. "All I know is I'm a better man for her."

My dearest Lenore,

If you're reading this letter, it's because I have finally slipped into the dark night that has been beckoning for so long now. I hope Tom is the one delivering the news to you. I hope you have the fortune to meet the wonderful man who made the last months of my life so full of love and life. Be kind to him, dear friend, for I think he will not come to you unbruised.

He loves me. And I love him. Most desperately.

He is, and will remain, my truest hero. My most dashing knight. The most honorable of scoundrels.

Remember me, Lenore. Remember our happy days at school and our silly rambles around town. Remember my stories. I hope they continue to bring joy to you and my readers. I wish there were more to leave behind, but I suppose I'd need a hundred years or more to write all the stories crowding my imagination. Twenty-nine was never going to be enough.

I've left them to you, my dearest editor, to do with as you please. I wasn't able to finish the grand story with the airships, but as you have a most excellent imagination, I know you will imagine a fine end for your favorite heroine. After all, I've given her your name.

I hope you find your own adventure. If there is one thing love has taught me, it is that one should never wait for life. Dare to live dangerously. You never know what mysteries could be waiting in the shadows.

I remain your true friend. Happy to the end. Content. And eager for the unknown embrace of night.

> Yours, always,
> Josephine Shaw Murphy

THE pretty, brown-haired woman set down the letter with tears in her eyes.

"Did she go peacefully?" she asked.

"Of course not," Tom said with a rueful smile. "Not Josie. She fought it, and I held her till the end."

A small sob escaped Miss Tetley's lips, and she covered her mouth with an embroidered handkerchief. Tom recognized Josie's slightly messy stitches on the edges.

"She was happy," Tom said. "She didn't linger long. Was active and writing up until two nights before she died. I'm happy for that."

Miss Tetley smiled. "She would have liked that. She could never be idle. A homebody, yes, but not an idle one. She loved working too much. There was always another book to read or a reference to check. A story to plan."

"She had great respect for you. And great affection. She spoke of you often."

"Thank you, Mr. Murphy. I am so sorry for your loss. Yet so happy you had the time with her that you did."

He nodded stiffly. "Thank you."

"Her father... it was only a few nights before that he died, wasn't it?"

"Yes. Only two nights."

"They were so very close."

"They were."

"Did..." She fidgeted a bit. "I know she was very keen that Mrs. Porter would receive the house in Bray, along with a generous allowance. Can you see that it be done? I hate to intrude, but Mrs. Porter—"

"Will be well looked after," Tom said. "Josie was very clear. I'm happy to see that she has a good retirement."

"Thank you, Mr. Murphy. I worried that Neville would make problems for you."

"Mr. Burke, as it happens, seems to have left Dublin. There's no sign of him at his usual haunts. There were rumors he'd fallen in with some disreputable companions."

"Oh." Miss Tetley's eyes widened. "How fortunate her father's business interests were transferred to your family then."

"We do not take the responsibility lightly, miss."

A few more polite exchanges left Tom feeling adrift. He had never been one for small talk—even less so when he felt as if he was lying—so he departed soon after Miss Tetley's father and mother returned from the theater. The young woman wiped her eyes and stood, clearly wrecked from grief but with a smile on her face.

"Thank you, Mr. Murphy, for delivering her letter and the books she left me. I'll treasure them."

"I'm glad."

"Will you be all right, sir?"

Tom paused. "I will never forget her. She was the most unexpected gift of my life. But she'd want me to keep going, wouldn't she?"

Miss Tetley nodded and gave him a brave smile. "She would."

A VERY PROPER MONSTER

"Then I'll be fine."

He put on his hat, tipped it toward her, and walked into the foggy London night.

THE house in Kinvara belonged to Anne. It was a great old farmhouse build up from a stone cottage that stood at the edge of Galway Bay. Most importantly, it was isolated. No humans lived around them for miles.

Like Tom, Josie had an affinity toward saltwater, which was lucky as the whole of Galway Bay was available for their play.

And they played.

They roamed the ocean, Josie buoyant with the joy of unexpected vitality. Tom often caught her breathing deeply as she sat in the salt air. She'd listen in wonder at the silence of her own lungs. Then a rare joy would cross her face, and she'd leap into the ocean, dancing beneath the water as if she were a mermaid.

Josie loved the sea. She told Tom she always had, though the doctors had warned her away from ocean-bathing when she'd been human. Now she held nothing back.

Her amnis was another story.

While Murphy and Declan were busy in Dublin, Anne had traveled out with them, hoping to help her friend along with learning to control her elemental strength. But even the most rudimentary lessons seemed to fail.

"Try again," Anne said, holding both of Josie's hands. "Do you feel it?"

"I do." Josie nodded. "It's sitting on the back of my

neck, moving over my shoulders, like water poured from a pitcher."

"Excellent. Now I want you to push it. Try to spread it over your skin. As if you were smoothing a stocking or pushing a glove up your arm."

Tom looked up from his newspaper, catching the small frown that grew between his wife's eyes.

"Are you trying?" Anne asked.

"I don't know," Josie said with a huff. "I can feel it, but it's not... It simply won't do what I want. I don't understand. Why is this so easy for all of you and not me?"

Anne sighed. It was their third lesson of the week, and so far, even the most rudimentary manipulation of amnis seemed beyond Josie. While a basic shield of amnis came instinctually for most vampires, it was not instinct to Josie.

"If you can't do this, you'll have no way of heating your skin," Anne said.

Josie shrugged. "Poor circulation? I can't see any humans for a long time anyway. Tom won't care, will you, Tom?"

"Course not," he grunted, trying not to be nosy. He didn't want to interfere with the lessons, after all. Just didn't want Anne to push his girl too far. She was still new at all this.

"And your skin will be too sensitive," Anne added.

"Sounds like an excellent reason to eschew fancy clothing." She winked at Tom, who only shook his head.

"Josie, you won't be able to hide forever," Anne said. "At some point, you'll have to rejoin society."

"Why?"

Tom blinked and looked up. "What do you mean, why?"

"Why will I need to rejoin society? Or at least public society." Her eyes were wide and guileless. "Will you need me to entertain for you?"

He snorted. "Not likely, love."

Anne said, "Tom's not much for company."

"Well, neither am I. I'd rather stay home and write. Perhaps read books or visit with family. Isn't that what I'll be doing for the foreseeable future anyway?"

Tom shrugged. "Sounds grand to my ears."

Anne said, "But... you'll be a hermit. You can't be a hermit. At least not forever."

"Why not?"

"Well, I..." Anne frowned. "You wouldn't be lonely?"

"I don't think so," Josie said. "We'll see. I never was much for company. And as long as I can go to the odd play or concert, walk in the park—"

"That'll be at night," Tom said. "No people around anyway."

"—and work in my garden with a friend every now and then, I think that's all I'll need. I love company, but only friends. I always hated formal parties."

Anne shook her head. "Good heavens, you two really are perfect for each other. Who would have guessed?"

"Me," Josie said with a sweet smile. "I knew we'd get on the first night he called on me."

Tom smiled and went back to his paper. Sweet butterfly girl...

"Oh?" Anne asked. "Why's that?"

"It was obvious," Josie said. "He brought me a book."

EPILOGUE

Dublin, 2015

JOSIE DUG INTO THE EARTH, feeling the coarse scrape of grit beneath her fingernails as she moved the loose soil from beneath the honeysuckle vine. The gardenia would be too overpowering, she thought. Perhaps the rosemary would provide a soothing note to balance the honeysuckle's sweet scent in the summer.

"Josie?" Tom called from the front of the garden.

"Come hither, my demon lover!"

His amused chuckle might have been her favorite sound in the world.

"Where do you want these roses?" he asked.

She turned and watched him as he placed one large pot down, then another. He'd stripped his shirt off and the misty night air clung to his muscled torso. His damp skin caught the light from the glass house he'd built her ten years ago.

He turned to her and caught her stare. "What?"

"You're a fine specimen of a man... for a monster."

"Am I?" He shook his head, his taciturn mouth never moving, though she caught the humor in his eyes. "Don't try to seduce me, fairy temptress. You'll never deter me from my mission."

She stabbed her trowel in the dirt and sat back, elbows propping her up as she turned innocent eyes toward him. "Your mission?"

"Yes." He swiped at the dew on his forehead, leaving a smear of dirt. "My lady has given me a task, and if I fail in it..." He sighed.

"She'd be disappointed?"

"Far worse than disappointed. Her fury would burn like the sun."

"Your lady sounds harsh, sir!"

"She is." He shook his head. "A right harridan. She beats me regularly."

"Oi!"

Tom finally broke into laughter. "Where do you want the roses?"

"One on either side, please." She pointed toward the willow in the corner. "Beats you regularly... I *should* beat you, ornery monster."

Josie didn't even hear him coming when he tackled her to the grass. She rolled across the lawn, laughing in his arms as Tom growled in her ear.

"I'll show you a monster." He nipped her ear and slowly scraped his fangs over her throat. "This monster has a taste for fair maiden. And look! Here's one sitting in my garden."

They wrestled in the grass until Josie was breathless from laughter. She threw her arms out and inhaled the fragrant night air, eyes closed and a satisfied smile on her face.

Tom reached out and traced her profile from her forehead, over her nose and down to her chin.

"Did you just smear dirt all over my face?"

"Yes. I've decided you're not a fair maiden. You're a warrior goddess, and this is your war paint."

"I like it. I could definitely write a story about a

warrior goddess."

"Josie..." He leaned over her, taking her lips in an achingly sweet kiss.

She smiled. "What?"

"Nothing," he murmured. "I just like saying your name is all."

"One of these days, Tom Dargin, I'm going to tell the world how sweet you are."

"No one'd believe you. Everyone knows writers are compulsive liars."

She burst into laughter again, and something about his expression, about the curve of his mouth just then, reminded her of the first time she'd seen him.

Solemn and serious, standing proud in her father's old house on Merrion Square. Telling her to stand up straight and never apologize for who she was, even if that was a rail-thin spinster with an overactive imagination and a withering cough.

And so it still was.

She adored him so much he could make her his slave. But then he wouldn't be the Tom who'd seen the quiet girl in the corner and asked her to stand tall, and Josie would be the caterpillar who never turned into a butterfly.

"I love you, Tom."

"Love you too, sweet girl."

"What a pair of monsters we are."

THE END

✝

AUTHOR'S NOTE

The book quoted in *A Very Proper Monster*—Josie's favorite story—is *Carmilla*, a vampire novella by Irish writer Joseph Sheridan Le Fanu. It was originally published in 1871 in the magazine *The Dark Blue* and later in his collection of short stories *In a Glass Darkly*.

Le Fanu's *Carmilla* predates Bram Stoker's classic vampire novel *Dracula* by over twenty-five years, and though lesser known, this influential story featured a female vampire who became the prototype for many important works in early vampire fiction and has been adapted or referenced many times in different media.

In a Glass Darkly is an early classic of Gothic literature and available for everyone through Project Gutenberg and major retailers.

NIGHT IN THE WAKING CITY
An Elemental World short story

O ✛ O

Chapter One

"I can't tell you what a pleasure it is to finally meet you," the young woman said. "I have to say, you're so much younger than I expected. Your body of work—"

"I love writing." Josie cut off the agent, quick to divert the conversation from anything that might cause the humans to question her visible age. "It's my favorite pastime as well as my job. And reading, of course. What's your favorite genre to read? Is it fantasy? Paranormal? I read everything. I'm on a historical mystery binge lately, and I'm enjoying it so much."

Tom Dargin smiled at his wife's deft diversion. She'd always been the clever one. He thumbed through the architectural magazine in the agent's office, waiting for Josie to finish her meeting.

She had been working with this agency in New York for nearly ten years, but this was the first time she'd ever agreed to a meeting. Tom and Josie rarely traveled from their home in Dublin for several reasons.

First, it was difficult for vampires to travel by

modern means. Tom was an enforcer for the vampire lord of Dublin, but he didn't have any fancy connections with specially fitted airplanes that could carry their kind. He and his mate traveled by boat, and crossing the Atlantic by boat was still a chore that took time.

Second, Tom worked. He wasn't a rich vampire of leisure, nor did he want to be. Though Josie made enough money for them to live in luxury, he still prided himself on being a working man. If he was a vampire who would live eternally, then work would be the thing that kept him sane.

Third, Josie was... Josie. Which meant she didn't like leaving her house and garden, much less her city or her country. He could count on one hand the number of times they'd traveled overseas in their one hundred thirty years together. And they'd only been to New York City once.

They'd traveled to the American city in the 1920s to spend the summer there, just after Josie had published a volume of poetry that had garnered some attention. The she met with an editor who had insulted her poetry and insinuated she was a rich dilettante who would only succeed if she slept with the right people. Him, to start.

Josie had left the editor's office like the dignified lady she was... only to track the man to his house later that night, drug him with opium, and kidnap him. She stripped the human naked and left him in Central Park to be found by irate constables in the morning. The man's professional reputation had never recovered, and Josie decided she didn't much like New York, despite the amusement.

Josie and the young agent named Carmen were

chatting about plans for a new gothic series when Tom heard another human enter the front office. There were two voices. The polite human who'd greeted them and another, louder one.

Josie stopped speaking and cocked her head slightly.

"I'm so sorry," Carmen said. "I have a writer who's just flown in from Europe and he wanted to go over a contract tonight. I told him I could meet with him after we were finished. I hope you don't mind."

"Not at all," Josie said, smiling to reassure the woman. "Shall we discuss the French translation offer? I'm not sure I want to go with the same house as last time. I wasn't at all pleased with their cover choices and they seemed very happy to ignore my calls."

Tom was surprised by the loud human in the front office, but he tried to remain outwardly impassive. He had thought they'd remain undisturbed; the unexpected visitor put his instincts on alert.

The voice was male. A smoker, by Tom's guess. The labored breathing didn't bode well for his health. And his voice was... arrogant. Tom wondered if the client chose to take late meetings because they were necessary or as a way of subtly manipulating those around him.

Josie *needed* to take meetings after dark. She explained it by citing a sun allergy—which was easy to believe with her pale, nearly translucent skin—and most agents and publishing professionals were quick to accommodate her.

The truth was she slept during daytime hours and would burn to a crisp in direct sunlight.

But Josie—or J.W. Shaw as she was known in this decade—was accepted as an eccentric, and her publisher didn't care because she sold so many books. The Shaw incarnation was a gothic mystery writer, the first time Josie had delved back into that type of literature since her human years. Gothic fiction was her first love, and in Tom's opinion, she was a master of it.

"Well, when *will* they be done?" the arrogant voice said from the outer office.

The voice was low enough that Carmen wouldn't hear, but Tom knew Josie would.

"Doesn't Carmen know I'm busy?" he continued. "I have *plans* tonight. Do you think it's easy to get reservations at The Polo Bar?"

Tom curled his lip. Carmen was in for a fun meeting. The man sounded like an arse.

As Josie and Carmen finished up, Tom heard footsteps coming down the book-lined hallway outside the office.

Oh, I don't think so.

Tom stood and walked to the door a moment before it swung open, blocking the entrance before the puffy-faced man burst in and disturbed his wife. The human looked to be in his mid-thirties and was dressed in black from head to toe. His hair was precisely styled to look unkempt. His skin and sour breath marked him as a heavy drinker. He was naturally thin, but desperately out of shape.

Tom crossed his arms over his chest and tipped up his jaw, looking down his nose at the human who hadn't expected to run into the living version of a brick wall.

"Can I help you?" Tom made sure his voice was Docklands rough. No need for niceties with this human.

The man tried to look around Tom, but had no

success. "I have a meeting with my agent. And who are you?"

"Think you're a bit early, lad. Why don't you wait at the front desk?"

Tom felt a gentle hand on his shoulder. He looked down and Josie was at his side.

"Carmen and I have just finished our meeting," she said diplomatically. "I believe you're Duncan Night, are you not? The paranormal romance writer?"

Duncan Night looked like he'd just smelled something awful. "I'd hardly classify my books as paranormal *romance*, because it's a genre and I don't write a *genre*. I write books delving into the psychological core of women as they grapple with the unknown. I write about women thrown into alien realities where they're forced to make sacrifices that could damn them or push them to the edge of a mortal precipice. I'd hardly call that paranormal romance."

Josie looked amused, which was good because Tom had the urge to punch the man's red-veined nose.

"I suppose not," she said. "Since someone inevitably dies at the end of all your books, that wouldn't exactly fit into standard genre norms."

Night sniffed. "Exactly."

"Plus, you're a man. I'm sure you're delving into territory that couldn't possibly have been covered by hundreds of talented female writers decades before you."

Tom didn't laugh at the sarcastic dig, but he wanted to.

Duncan Night curled his lip, his eyes ran up and down Josie, appraising her. "And who are you?"

"J.W. Shaw," Josie said. "I write gothic mystery. The

Evangeline Edwards series? I believe my latest book was just above yours on the bestseller list last week."

The man's eye twitched. "I've never heard of you. I don't really look at lists."

Tom nearly snorted. Josie was looking amused, which was why the man was still standing, ignorant of his own "mortal precipice."

"Of course you don't," she said. "I'm sure only *genre* writers pay attention to things like lists."

"And who is this?" Night glanced at Tom. "Your bodyguard?"

"My husband," Josie said.

"Another bored housewife writing drivel," Night muttered. "Typical."

Well, that did it. Tom threw an arm around Josie's shoulders as her fangs dropped, herding her from the office as visions of opium and blood splatter filled his mind's eye. "Nice to meet you, Carmen," he called. "We'll see you next time."

Or not.

"Ms. Shaw!" Carmen followed them down the hall, desperate to repair the situation. "If you could give me a call before you leave the city—"

"Sure thing," Tom said. He shielded Josie from the eyes of the secretary. He could smell blood and wondered if his mate had bitten her own lip. Tom could feel her irregular amnis jumping and sparking against his skin. "I'll make sure she does that." *Right after I make sure she doesn't murder Duncan Night.*

Chapter Two

Typical.

Josie sat in the backseat of the hired car with Tom at her side.

Steady Tom. Lovely Tom. Responsible Tom. Tom who had kept her from slicing the neck of the trashy writer who liked to pretend he shocked everyone by the twisted deaths at the end of his books. The writer who had called *her*, Josephine Shaw, also known as Joseph Doyle, Viviana Dioli, J.W. Shaw, and a dozen other pen names... typical.

Typical?

"I was a bestseller before his grandparents were born," she said.

"He's full of shite," Tom said. "Say it with me, Jo. 'Duncan Night is full of shite.' It even rhymes."

"As if that's his real name. *Duncan Night.* My arse. He's full of shite, all right." She paused. "You're right, it does rhyme. Why is that irritating?"

"It's not irritating, it's funny."

"He called me typical."

"Which you're not."

She whipped around to face him. She could still feel her fangs, long in her mouth. "Why do I care?"

"I don't know." Tom reached over and grabbed her hand, bringing it to his lips to kiss her knuckles. "You shouldn't."

"Besides, what does he know about being a housewife? I've been a housewife, and it's anything but boring."

Tom narrowed his eyes. "I'd hardly call you a housewife."

"Why not?" Josie said. "I'm a wife. I work at home. That's a housewife, Tom."

"I suppose you're right."

"And it's damn hard to run a house," Josie said. "It's fecking hard work. I'd like to see that arsehole manage the proper running of a house."

"I doubt that man properly runs at all," Tom said. "Again, why do you care?"

"I don't!" She tasted blood and knew she'd bitten her own lip again.

"Right," Tom said quietly.

They both fell silent, and Josie was glad the divider was up between the driver and the passengers. The driver was human, and when she was angry, she didn't *always* exhibit the best self-control.

"Doesn't write in a genre," she muttered.

"Jo..."

"He *does* write in a genre," she said. "It's a genre called 'predictable sexist shite.' Trust me, he's hardly the first writer to publish in it."

"Quite right."

"I was *complimenting* him when I said paranormal romance. He doesn't deserve the title."

"Romance is one of the oldest genres of literature," Tom said. "And the most widely read for a reason. You know I love a good romance."

"I know you do," she said. "Because you're a smart man, Tom."

He smiled. "Thank you, sweet girl."

"A smart man who doesn't buy into the sexist rubbish *that* human needs to feel good about his sad, pathetic career!"

"Is this calming you down or riling you up?" Tom asked.

"I can't tell yet."

"Because I know something that's guaranteed to calm you down *and* rile you up." Tom leaned over and whispered something dirty and decadent that had her squirming in her seat.

"Are you trying to distract me with sex?" Josie asked.

"Yes."

"As I just said... you're a very smart man."

Tom sucked hard on her inner thigh, easing her into another climax before he pulled back, smacked her bottom with his palm, and slid up her body and into her in one smooth movement. He was big and rough and Josie loved it. She loved how broad his shoulders were. How she could dig her nails into them and he'd only grunt and growl and bite her harder.

She loved that he'd taken her back to their hotel, then taken her against a wall, driving any thought of bloody revenge from her mind. Then he'd thrown her in a warm shower and teased her for an hour before he brought her back to the bed. They were on hour four, and the manic energy that had riled her was finally easing away.

Her mate had driven it away with pleasure.

Tom braced himself over her and rocked his hips. He was silent, which meant he was waiting for Josie to look at him. She opened her eyes and looked up.

"I love you," she whispered with a smile.

Oh, the look in his eyes.

"I *adore* you," Josie reached up and cupped his scarred face. "You are my life. My eternity. I love you so much, Tom."

He groaned and his stern look collapsed in pleasure. He kissed her hard when he came, then he buried his face in her neck as she ran her hands up and down his back. He licked the bite he'd made on her neck when he took her against the wall. He breathed deeply, and she knew he was taking in the scent of their mingled blood.

One hundred thirty years she'd loved this man. One hundred thirty years he'd been her mate and protector.

Josie knew she wasn't a normal vampire, but Tom loved her anyway.

Her skin was cold unless her mate excited her. She'd never been able to control her amnis like others did. She sometimes flew into rages or fugues. She often saw things she wasn't sure were real or a dream.

But Tom was always there. Always protecting her. Always watching.

She ran her fingernails through the short clip of his hair as he lay stretched over her like a great cat. She could almost feel him purring. Tom was a man who craved affection, but would never ask for it.

He didn't have to. She knew him.

Tom rolled them to the side, still buried in her, and dragged her leg over his. Josie pressed her mouth against his chest and nipped at his skin. Goosebumps rose on his arms. He pressed a hand to the small of her back and shifted his hips. He was still hard.

"You going to sleep like this today, Josie-girl?" Tom pinched her bottom and gripped the back of her thigh to angle her tighter against him. "Sleep with my hard cock in you? Wake up like this so I can make love to you while you feed from me at nightfall?"

Her earlier anger was gone. Forgotten. Barely a memory.

"You are very, very good at distracting me."

"Just doing my job, Ms. Shaw."

Josie smiled and knew her fangs would stay down all night.

Chapter Three

Tom took the stairs to the fourth floor of their hotel. It was called a "boutique property," according to Cormac O'Brien, the vampire he'd been meeting with that night. Just because he was here for Josie's meeting didn't mean he couldn't accomplish a bit of business for his boss. Tom knew the meeting would only take an hour, then he'd have the rest of the night with Josie.

New York City was run by a cabal of vampires from the clan O'Brien. They were earth vampires running an island, which was unusual in itself. The fact that they were also crooks wasn't unusual, but the fact that they were attempting to transition to legitimate business was.

The "boutique property" where Tom and Josie were staying was one of their investments. Declan had come to the United States the year before to oversea the installation of the Nocht voice recognition system that allowed the hotel to be modern while still being vampire friendly. The system waited for Tom to enter an old fashioned key in the lock, then did a facial recognition scan before he was allowed to enter the suite.

"Josie?" he called. "Finished with work. You ready to go out?"

He walked down the hall, setting his keys on the table. He and Josie had a leisurely nightfall. They'd fed from each other, then enjoyed some blood wine before he'd left. She was talking about trying to find a late show they could see together if Tom returned in time.

"Jo?" He didn't hear her. Didn't smell her. His heart thumped once. "Josie-girl?"

Josie didn't always register to normal vampire senses because of her abnormal amnis, but it was rare for Tom to have trouble finding her. He kept his breathing even and checked the suite. She wasn't there. He didn't see a note.

Josie never went out without him. Not when she was in her right mind.

Damn.

There was a paper laying open on the coffee table. Tom walked over and examined it. It was open to the Arts section, and he saw a few show listings circled on one side.

Then he saw the article opposite the show listings.

For a book signing at a bookstore in Union Square.

A book signing with Duncan Night.

His stomach dropped, but he kept his voice steady. "Nocht system engage."

"Welcome to Nocht." A pleasant voice with a clear Irish accent spoke. "How can I assist you, Tom Dargin?"

He retrieved a small black cube from his briefcase. "Nocht personal encryption system engage. Client 6241886."

There were a few moments of silence, then a buzzing sound. A different voice spoke. "Welcome to the Nocht Encryption System, Client 6241886. Please wait for scan."

Tom stepped away from the cube, which glowed with a low light. He didn't know what exactly it did, but something about the process made his amnis wake up. The water in the air drew to his skin for a moment, then the cube when black again and there was another quiet buzzing sound.

"Your room has been scanned and cleared. Please confirm personal identification code."

"Five-one-seven-two-four."

"Please confirm password."

"Carmilla."

"Thank you." There was a moment of silence, then his personal digital assistant spoke in a lower male voice. "Good evening, Tom. How can I assist you tonight?"

"Please connect me to Brigid Connor on her encrypted line."

There were another few moments of silence, during which Tom tried to remain calm. He'd only been gone an hour and a half. She couldn't have gone far. But he needed local help before he went hunting for her. Someone he could trust. Someone discreet. Someone not in the employ of the O'Briens, who would not take kindly to a possibly unbalanced vampire hunting bestselling novelists in their city. Even if those bestselling novelists were complete arseholes.

"Tom?" Brigid's voice on the line.

"We may have a problem. Josie's gone."

"*What?*"

"Who do we know in New York City? Who can we trust?"

She was silent for a moment. "Okay. I may have an idea, but you'll have to hear me out."

Chapter Four

Carwyn was on the speakerphone while Ben sorted his vinyl collection. Was it a hipster pretension? Maybe. Or maybe he just liked records.

"I don't think I've met this guy," Ben said. "What's he doing in New York again?"

"You've not met him," Carwyn said, "but Tom Dargin is a very old friend of Murphy's and a close friend of Brigid's. He needs help finding his wife and you're going to help him."

Ben hated being ordered around, even by Carwyn. "We don't really find *people*. That's not our thing."

"Well, it is tonight."

He glanced up to see Tenzin peeking out of her loft. "Are you going to chime in here?"

"We don't find people, Carwyn."

Carwyn huffed in frustration. "That's the most ridiculous thing I've heard, especially from you, Tenzin. I know you're a self-indulgent pain-in-the-ass most of the time, but look at this as an opportunity to gain a favor from someone useful."

Tenzin shrugged and went back to her cave. "Whatever. It could be entertaining."

There was a knock at the door.

"That would be Tom," Carwyn said.

"You gave him our address?" Ben said. "What the

hell, Carwyn?"

"*Benjamin.*"

It was rare for Carwyn to use the priest voice, but he still occasionally did it. And it still made Ben feel like he was fifteen. He put down the records and listened.

Carwyn continued, his voice low and deadly. "You will stop whatever you're in the middle of right now and help Tom Dargin. You'll do this as a personal favor to me, and because this is a man you should know. A favor to him will not be wasted. Do you understand me?"

It rankled, but he said, "Fine."

Tenzin flew down from her loft and walked to the door. "Don't worry. I'm very good at finding people."

Carwyn said, "Between the two of you, you should be able to find her without too much mayhem."

"Wow." Ben stood and brushed off his pants. "Thanks for the vote of confidence, Father."

"Go help Tom," Carwyn said. "Thank me for the introduction later."

Ben walked to the door while Tenzin opened it, his hands in his pockets.

Whoever he was expecting to walk in, it wasn't a giant brute of a vampire who looked like an extra from a British mobster movie. This vampire was over six feet tall and looked like a human version of a semi-truck. His face was scarred and his jaw looked like it had been broken more than once.

"Hello," Tenzin said. "You must be Tom Dargin."

"I am." Dargin narrowed his eyes on Tenzin. "You don't look like a Benjamin Vecchio, but I'm not one to judge. You the one Brigid said could help me?"

"I'm Ben." He walked over, hands still in his pockets.

He wasn't keen on shaking hands with unknown vampires. "This is Tenzin. She's my partner."

Dargin recognized the name, but the recognition was tempered by the clear worry on his face. "I need help finding my wife."

"Why'd she run away?" Tenzin asked.

"She didn't run away. Precisely."

Ben motioned to the chairs in front of the television. "Let's sit and you can tell us what's going on."

"I'd rather not," Dargin said. "She's already on the move and she's fast."

Oh shit. What had Carwyn gotten Ben into? He wasn't in the habit of hunting down rogue vampires.

Tenzin's face was no longer amused. "What is her element?"

"Water."

"Who is she hunting?"

"A writer named Duncan Night. Do you know him?"

Tenzin made a face. "His books are awful. I don't understand why so many people buy them. Someone always dies at the end."

"I don't read him," Ben said. "But I know who it is. Gavin had to ban him from a club a few months ago."

"Josie, my wife, is also a writer and Night insulted her last night," Dargin said. "I thought she'd forgotten about it, but..."

"She's that easily offended?" Ben said. "Most vampires—"

"Josie's not most vampires." Dargin grimaced. "It's hard to explain. She was turned when she was very ill. I don't know what Brigid told you, but she's a wonderful girl. Normally she's a very gentle person, but sometimes... I doubt she'd kill him, but she's not always clear about who she is. Or what she is. She's not cruel, but an... incident of some kind is definitely possible. And you probably know how the O'Briens feel about public scenes."

"The O'Briens are paranoid as hell." Ben sighed. "Do you have any idea where she's going?"

"A bookstore on Union Square. Night had a signing tonight that started at nine."

"Would she attack in front of humans?" Tenzin asked.

"I doubt it. She'd try to get him on his own."

Tenzin nodded. "My kind of girl."

Dargin frowned. "I'm not sure—"

"Where was she coming from?" Ben asked. Better that Dargin didn't question Tenzin too closely.

"Not far from here. We're staying at a place in the West Village."

Ben could see Tenzin doing the mental calculations. "I'll fly." Without a backward glance, she went to the French doors leading to the roof garden, walked outside, and disappeared into the night.

Dargin turned to Ben. "Is that who I think it is?"

"Yes."

"And she lives with you?"

Ben shrugged. "As much as she lives anywhere."

Dargin snorted. "Good luck with that one."

"Oh yeah?" Ben grabbed a messenger bag and walked to the door. "Not taking advice from a guy who lost his wife."

Dargin's expression turned stormy. "Watch yourself, Vecchio. I'm not a forgiving kind of vampire. I don't care who your uncle is or who your partner is. I'm after my wife. You can either help me or stay out of my way. I don't have time for a young man's ego."

Ben considered leaving him to find his wife on his own. But... it was actually refreshing to interact with a vampire who wasn't awed by his uncle or by Tenzin. "You don't know this city. I do. I'll help you, and you'll owe me one."

Dargin held out his hand and Ben took it. "Fair enough. Help me find Josie, and I'll owe you a favor all your own."

Chapter Five

She watched the human blink as he woke. He'd been snoring for roughly two hours, and with each snore, the pulsing of his carotid artery seemed to get louder. Would severe blood loss make him stop snoring? There was only one way to find out.

But he didn't smell good. If he'd smelled good, she would have already drunk from him. He didn't, so she waited for the stench of alcohol to drift away. It permeated his skin. Made her recoil in disgust. It was harsh and sour.

She liked wine. She craved it sometimes. She craved it now.

She was thirsty and she wanted to drink.

No, sweet girl.

She blinked.

No, she shouldn't drink. Not from him.

Why not?

Tom wouldn't like it.

Tom?

That's right. She wanted to make Tom happy. It was important to make Tom happy.

Watch it! Watch him.

She *had* watched him.

She'd keep watching him. That would make Tom happy.

The insipid human had been so easy to find, sitting in the front of that bookstore, his ego incandescent in the pale florescent lights. Josie had never done a book signing. They wanted her to, but Tom said she couldn't. Not even at night. It wasn't a good idea. Pictures lasted forever now.

But this human could sign books. He signed many of them. And yet Josie could tell he didn't respect his readers. She could see his veiled disgust as ordinary people, who'd waited for hours in line and bought his awful books, took their turn to meet him. She saw the fake smiles and the disdain.

I should bite him.

No.

Josie was tired of watching him. She slapped his cheek hard. "Wake up."

His eyes flew open. "What? Where am I?"

It was a good question.

Where are you, Josie?

Empty flat. That's right. No lights on. Wine on the table. She tasted apple on her tongue and the memory of it jogged the memory of a tree at home.

Apple trees in the garden...

"Taste, sweet girl."

Tom liked apples.

"Who are you? Where am I?" the man asked again.

The human's name was fake. It was a fake name.

She had many fake names.

Duncan Night. That was his fake name.

There was a buzzing in the back of her mind. She felt surges of heat against her skin like waves that ebbed and rose. The water in the air drew to her. Drifted away.

Drew to her again. Then drifted away. She shook her head, trying to clear her mind.

"Who are you?" the man said.

"There are"—she blinked her eyes— "a startlingly large number of empty flats in this city."

"I don't understand." His words were slurred.

She wondered if it had been coffee in that mug on the signing table. Judging by the smell of the alcohol—

"You were drinking whiskey." No wonder she hadn't tasted him yet. She didn't like whiskey.

"What if I was?" Night said.

So disdainful, even with a creature like her, a monster who could kill him so easily.

So very easily...

She leaned forward, but his smell hit her again. She backed away. "Tom wouldn't like it."

"Who?"

Her head was pounding. And clearing.

Oh dear...

Josie glanced around the apartment. Duncan Night was sitting on a kitchen chair, his arms slack at his sides. There was a bottle of something on the table and a handkerchief. She could smell chloroform in the air.

Josie sighed. "Oh... damn."

Night was stammering and confused. "Who...? H-how?"

Josie put a hand over her face. Flashes of the night were coming back to her like pictures flipping in her mind. "You were pathetically easy to track." Her stomach roiled from the combined smell of the chloroform and the alcohol in his breath. "You should practice awareness of the world around you, Duncan, and not look at your phone so much. Humans look at their phones too often. It makes them vulnerable."

His eyes were open and his jaw was slack, but she couldn't tell if he remembered her. "Who are you?"

"Obviously, I'm the woman who kidnapped you."

Night groaned. "Oh my God. Oh God, it finally happened. You an insane reader, aren't you?"

Josie was confused. "What?"

"You're going to keep me locked away until I write some book for you. Or rewrite an ending or something. Or you think you're in love with me and—"

"Oh Jaysus, stop. You're obnoxious." Josie felt her amnis trickle across her skin. "And you flatter yourself. You're a horrible writer. I'd never kidnap you to make you write something for me. Get your head out of your arse."

Night's eyes were bloodshot. He reeked of alcohol and sweat. "Why—?"

"You really don't remember me?" Josie asked. Her revulsion for the man dusted the last of the cobwebs from her mind.

Why had she taken this smelly human again?

Josie rubbed her temple. She'd been so angry the night before. Why had she been angry?

The human squinted. "Wait... you're the writer. The one at Carmen's office. The housewife with the giant husband."

Oh, that's right. Josie's nostril's flared. She felt her fangs drop down. "Another bored housewife writing drivel? Isn't that what you said?"

Night's face went pale. "Oh God."

"That's right." Josie smiled. "You remember me

now."

"Ohmygod. I'm h-hallucinating," he stammered. "Someone drugged me."

Had she?

Shit. She had. Tom was going to be so angry.

Still... this man was a horrible arse. He needed someone to give him a talking-to. As long as she had him terrified...

"Yes, I drugged you." *Be the scary vampire, Josie. Remember, you* are *a monster.* "I couldn't have you making a scene in public, could I?"

"You have fangs," Night whispered. "You have fangs."

Play it cool. She reached up and touched her fangs. "That's right. I do." She leapt across the room and bent over him. "But you write about creatures with fangs, Duncan. You should know they're real."

"Not real. Not real. Not real," he chanted.

She could smell his urine puddle on the floor.

"That's not nice, Duncan. This isn't your apartment. Have some manners."

Bullies always pissed themselves when they were confronted. *Remember Cousin Neville?*

For a moment, she was back in the smoky bedroom. She tasted Neville's blood on her tongue.

So sweet...

The human's heart was racing. She leaned toward him, her mouth watered when she heard the blood. It was right there...

And it smelled. She shook her head and backed away.

Thank goodness Duncan Night reeked so much of

whiskey. If his blood was sweeter, she knew she'd be explaining more than a kidnapping.

Oh, Tom was going to be so angry. And Josie had been hoping to stay in New York long enough to see Hamilton if they could bribe someone for tickets. She stood and paced in front of Night.

Had Tom told the O'Briens? Probably not. Now that the bloodlust had died down, she needed to figure out what to do with this awful man so she could get back to their hotel.

"This is a bad trip," he chanted. "It's just a bad trip."

Josie patted his cheek. It wasn't exactly a slap, but it got his attention. "I want to talk to you, Duncan. Pay attention."

He started to cry. "Are you going to kill me?"

"Probably not."

"What do you want from me?"

"As I said, I want to talk." She pulled up a chair and sat down across from him. The man had his arms plastered to his sides. Josie squinted. "You know, I haven't tied you up."

He lifted his arms and stared at them, as if he'd only just realized he wasn't bound. Then he looked back at Josie.

Yep. Still terrified.

Well, since she had him here... Josie folded her hands together and put them on her crossed knees. "So, Duncan, let's talk about your writing. How does it feel to be in an 'alien reality?' Isn't this what you write?"

He just shook his head.

"Unfamiliar genre?" she asked. "Or is this situation only worthy of examination when you have a helpless female protagonist under your control? Have you been 'pushed to the edge of a mortal precipice' yet?"

"What do you want from me?"

Nothing. I want to go home and forget this happened.

But since you're here...

"I want you to think, Duncan. It's not just that you're a bad writer. You have several problems we need to cover. For instance, you only write about women in peril. And they're *very* one-dimensional. It's lazy characterization. Or is it some sick fantasy you have? Is this some strange compulsion to put women in danger?" She leaned forward and bared her fangs. "That's not very nice."

"Okay, I'll stop." He started to cry. "Is that what you want?"

"I want you to stop being such a pretentious arse. Do you really think you're doing anything different from the thousands of talented female romance authors out there? No, you just have a penis, so reviewers think you're special. But you're not. Really, you're not. What you are is a lazy plotter. Killing characters solely for shock value is lazy plotting, Duncan."

He nodded. "I know."

"But you just keep doing it. Why do you keep doing it?"

"I'll stop. I promise. I'll write a happily-ever-after. I promise you. Everyone will live."

Going on impulse, Josie reached out and put a hand on his forearm. "You're not *really* going to stop, are you?"

Night's eyes crossed and Josie realized her amnis

was actually doing something. *Interesting.*

"No," he slurred. "I'm not going to stop."

"I didn't think so." She pulled her hand back and watched as his mind cleared.

"*What did you do to me?*"

"I have no idea."

Night started to cry. It was messy and ugly. His face got very red and his nose ran.

"Stop crying."

He cried harder.

Josie curled her lip. "You're letting snot drip down your chin. It's disgusting."

Night used his shirt to wipe his nose. He seemed to get some courage back and his eyes hardened. "I remember you. *J.W. Shaw.* I know who you are. You better let me go, or I'll—"

"What?" She crouched front of him, moving inhumanly fast, baring her fangs. "What are you going to do, Duncan? Tell on me? Who do you think would believe you?"

Typical. She gives a man perfectly valid writing feedback, and he threatens her.

"You're an arrogant pissant, Duncan Night. And probably an alcoholic. I'd talk to someone about that if I were you."

"You're a *vampire!*"

"I know!"

"I'm not hallucinating. I'm not dreaming. You're real." His lower lip trembled. "Aren't you?"

"Oh, I'm very real." Josie sat back in her chair. "Now, let's talk about your redundant descriptions. Because I know your editor is not letting you get away with that.

Which means you're ignoring your editor, Duncan. And there's really no excuse for it."

He whispered, "Just tell me. Are you going to kill me?"

"I don't know. Are *you* going to keep abusing adverbs?"

Chapter Six

Tenzin stopped by the bookstore first. There was no sign of the human writer, though she'd been able to take a mental picture of Duncan Night from the large poster still standing in the corner, along with drawing in a good whiff of the human's distinctive scent. She'd read his books, but she'd never noticed what he looked like.

Night's book weren't very good, and Tenzin could always guess who the writer was going to kill about thirty percent into the book.

And he *always* killed someone. Not even Tenzin had a record that lethal.

Even more irritating, they were never *good* deaths. No one ever fell nobly in battle. There was rarely even courageous sacrifice. No, Duncan Night wrote stupid deaths. An otherwise competent sailor taking off into a storm. A doctor with cancer who should have caught it early enough to treat. Drivers who had accidents on slippery roads driving after someone they could have called on the telephone.

Stupid deaths. Very irritating. She'd stopped reading after the third book.

Still, bad writing was not a mortal offense.

Tenzin overheard two of the store clerks talking about the signing and decided to listen in for a few minutes.

"Such an jerk," one muttered. "'This coffee is too hot. This coffee is too cold.'"

The other joked, "That coffee was just right as soon as he got some booze into it."

Both of them laughed, ignoring Tenzin, who pretended to read a book on the shelf.

"How many people do you think tonight?"

"Sheila said there were two hundred that checked out with his stuff."

"He's an ass, but I guess he sells books."

"They're making a movie about the one that came out last year."

"Don't they make movies of all of them?"

The employee groaned. "Yeah. And they're all total crap."

"You know... I heard J.W. Shaw was in town yesterday."

"I'll believe it when I see it. She never does signings."

"They say she was meeting with her agent or something."

"Do you know how many writers and agents live in lower Manhattan? I think even Sir Pompous McWhiskeybreath lives in the Village somewhere. If Shaw was here, we'll probably never know. The woman is a complete mystery."

Tenzin was guessing McWhiskeybreath referred to Duncan Night. She slipped out of the bookstore and walked toward the Village. It was more likely the writer had taken a cab, but sometimes drunks liked to walk. And Duncan Night certainly sounded like a drunk.

Tenzin *had* to walk because it wasn't dark enough to fly comfortably and the buildings on University Place were short enough that she'd be noticed from the ground.

Half a block north of Washington Square Park, she caught his scent. It was the same as the human in the bookstore, and it was just as unpleasant. She followed it past the Washington Mews and along the north side of the park. Halfway along the north side of the park, she also scented a hint of chloroform.

Curious.

Most vampires would be able to make a human fall unconscious or even control one just by touch, which meant Tom Dargin must not have been lying about his wife's amnis. Tenzin had to admit she'd been skeptical, but apparently it was true. Josie Shaw had uncontrollable amnis.

It was interesting. And not much was interesting to Tenzin.

The chloroform joined the human's scent on Waverly Place. Tenzin slowed down and opened her senses.

Duncan Night. Chloroform. A sweet note of jasmine.

And the acrid tang of adrenaline and urine.

Found you.

No blood. That was good.

Duncan Night was a bad writer, but she didn't want to worry about cleaning up a body.

Tenzin walked to the alleyway behind an apartment building and flew up, trying to pinpoint the location. She heard a woman's voice and landed softly on the fire escape.

"...let's talk about your redundant descriptions. Because I know your editor is not letting you get away with that. Which means you're ignoring your editor,

Duncan. And there's really no excuse for it."

"Just tell me. Are you going to kill me?"

"I don't know. Are *you* going to keep abusing adverbs?"

Tenzin burst out laughing.

It was a very valid question.

There was a pause, then the sound of footsteps running. A thin, dark-haired woman poked her head out of a window. "Who are you?"

"Tenzin. Are you Josie?"

The look of relief was evident. "Yes. Did Tom send you?"

"Tom sent me."

"Thank God." She waved her in. "Wind vampire or excellent climber?"

"Wind vampire." Tenzin flew to the window and crawled through. She stopped just inside. "You're not tied up," she said to the human. "You didn't even try to run?"

"He's very passive," Josie said. "Which is another problem, Duncan. Your use of the passive voice is dire. I'm not one of those writers who insists on *never* using it, but you go much too far. Again, lazy."

Tenzin said. "And I fully agree with her point about adverbs. You use *very* or *much* in nearly every sentence."

Duncan Night's face was white. "Oh my God, there's another one."

Tenzin grinned and winked. "And my fangs are always down."

Josie said, "Are they really? That's fascinating."

"Yes." Tenzin cocked her head. "What is wrong with your amnis? It's very strange."

163

"Oh!" Josie smiled. "It's quite refreshing that you just asked. Most people don't."

"I'm often told I have problems with boundaries."

"It doesn't bother me," Josie said. "I was turned when I was quite ill. Nearly out of my mind. I get a bit... fuzzy sometimes. It's gotten better over the years. I think the more blood Tom and I exchange, the better it gets."

"That's interesting."

"It is." Josie put her hands on her hips. "But also problematic. I don't know what to do with him. I can't wipe his memory, you see. And Tom will be very cross about all this."

"I wouldn't worry about it. I think he'll be relieved you didn't kill him."

"Oh, I haven't done that in years."

Tenzin shrugged. "Should be fine then. But you're right. What do we do with this one?" She crouched down in front of Duncan Night of the horrible novels and grinned. "I do have a few ideas."

Chapter Seven

Tom walked with the young human around the wrought iron fencing of Stuyvesant Square Park. Nothing. No sign of her. He was starting to worry, but Ben had been checking the police radio and said there had been no reports of violence or mayhem around Union Square, which gave Tom some degree of comfort.

"We had a house here in the 1920s," Tom said, pointing ahead of them. "Just over there."

"It's a cool neighborhood."

"Cool. Right." Tom nodded. "We had interesting neighbors. Josie loved it for a while."

"Only a while?"

"A book person of some kind insulted her. She took her revenge quite publicly and ruined his career. He might have ended up naked in Central Park." Tom smiled. "She decided she missed Dublin after that."

Ben laughed out loud. "I think I'll like Josie."

There was a knot in the middle of his belly. "She's quite likable."

She's quite everything.

What if one of the O'Brien found her? What if someone else did? When Josie was in a state, she could be innocent as a lamb or lost in a rage. It was totally unpredictable, and she had no concept of secrecy.

Or consequences.

She'd be gutted if she did anything to harm the man. Her temper could be a fierce thing, but when she came back to herself, she'd be wrecked with guilt if she did any permanent harm. Tom thought she'd been getting better. He'd thought the rages weren't so quick to take her these days. She had dreams and fugues, of course, but the violence she'd struggled with in her youth had lessened.

Hadn't it?

The young human was quiet. Tom strained to listen, but there was nothing but traffic and the common noises of the city at night.

"No scent of her?" Ben asked. "She's your mate."

"It doesn't work like that for us. It never has. Her amnis recognizes mine, but only when I'm close."

"So she's not in this neighborhood?"

He shook his head. "I was hoping she might come back here because it was familiar."

Ben paused on the sidewalk and Tom stopped beside him.

"I vote we walk back toward Union Square," Ben said. "Tenzin has probably already found her. She's looking from the air and she's an incredibly good tracker. And if she hadn't, she'd have gone back to the apartment and used Cara to call me."

"Are you sure?"

Ben shrugged. "I'm never sure of anything with Tenzin, but I'm guessing that's what she'd do. And I've worked with her for about five years now."

"Fine." He didn't really have a choice. "We head back to Union Square. From there, we'll go back to your apartment. We can pass by the human's flat on the way, isn't that right?"

"We can. He lives on the north end of Greenwich Village. You can keep looking for Josie with your mate voodoo while we walk."

"Fine," he said.

Tom would live with Ben's plan, because it was the only thing keeping him sane. They started walking west on East 14th Street, and Tom kept his senses alert for any signs of Josie.

"You've worked with Tenzin for some time," he said. "You truly think she's found her?"

"It's likely. She was an assassin for centuries, she can fly, and she's very sneaky. I tend to bet on sneaky."

Tom decided to believe Ben. The other options didn't suit him, and he had to believe that even if the little air vampire hadn't found Josie, his sweet girl would have snapped out of her rage by now. The rages didn't last forever. Whatever the fallout was, they'd deal with it. Hopefully, it wouldn't be too painful. The O'Briens owed Murphy a few favors anyway. And Murphy owed Tom more than he could count.

Tom made conversation so he wouldn't go mad. "So when do you plan on turning?" he asked. "Will Tenzin sire you or your uncle? I'm not going to assume what's going on there so—"

"I'm not going to become a vampire," Ben said.

Tom frowned. "That's ridiculous. All your people are vampires, aren't they?"

"That doesn't mean I have to be one."

Tom muttered, "Selfish."

"Selfish?" Ben said. "Did you say I'm *selfish*?"

"Yes."

Ben curled his lip. "You know what? It's not any of

your business."

"I suppose not." Tom shrugged. "Doesn't make you any less selfish."

"Did you *choose* to become a vampire?"

"Yes."

"Well, as far as I'm concerned, I get to choose, too."

"You'll choose what you want," Tom said. "I'm not going to change your mind. But when my best friend in the world gave me the option of growing old and dying or joining him and being part of his family, I did what any decent friend would do and stayed with the people I loved."

"It's not that simple," Ben said. "I know what your world is like."

"I'm sure you do." Tom saw the lights of Union Square ahead. "But if you don't want this life, then why are you in it? I don't see anyone keeping you prisoner."

"You're saying if I'm going to be around vampires, I have to be one?" Ben asked. "That's ridiculous. Doesn't Murphy have his day people?"

"There's a difference between day people and what you are." Tom paused at the light and turned to Ben. "We all have to learn to say goodbye to humans we care about. That's part of immortal life. But what you are, is family. So yes, if you turn your back on that, you're selfish."

"I don't agree."

"You don't want this life? Walk away. Give them distance before you die." The light changed and Tom started across. "You stay, that means you want it, whether you admit it or not."

The young human didn't say anything, but that was

fine. It wasn't Tom's job to be his teacher. He'd learn. Or he'd lose.

Tom just hoped he wasn't the one losing his mind before the night was done.

Chapter Eight

The human was trembling all over. "You're going to kill me," he said. "You're going to—"

"Did I say I was going to kill you?" Tenzin said.

Duncan Night shook his head.

"Then be quiet. If I start killing you, you have permission to scream." Tenzin stood from her crouch.

Josie was leaning against a couch, not sure what to make of the strange vampire who'd found her. She couldn't decide if Tenzin was sixteen or thirty. She had an American accent, but that didn't mean anything with vampires. Many took on accents the way they changed clothes. The small wind vampire felt incredibly powerful. And very old.

But Tom had sent her, so she had to be safe.

"I am so sorry about this," Josie said.

"Don't be! I wasn't doing anything interesting tonight. And Ben was just organizing his records."

"Who's Ben?"

"The human I live with."

"Boyfriend?"

Tenzin wrinkled her nose. "No, he's young, but I don't think he'd be considered a boy anymore."

"That's not exactly what I..." Talking with Tenzin felt a little like being in an altered state. "I'm not sure who you are. Do you know Tom from work?"

"No. I'm an independent contractor. Not under anyone's aegis, but we're friends with Carwyn and Brigid. Ben and I find things."

"Things?"

Tenzin smiled her fangy smile. "And tonight we find people! I used to find people a long time ago. To kill them. But I don't do that anymore."

Josie couldn't decide if she was more horrified or fascinated.

Duncan Night was horrified. "Oh my God. Oh my God, I'm going to die."

"Not like this one, though." Tenzin bent over. "You kill characters the way some people lose socks. What is wrong with you?"

"They're just stories."

"Stories are important."

"I know they are."

"So stop killing all the interesting characters. And if you need to kill someone, give them a *good* death."

Duncan Night looked confused. "O-okay."

The scale tottering between horror and fascination fell firmly on the fascinated side. Josie didn't know what to make of Tenzin, but she decided she definitely liked her, and whoever she was, Josie wanted to be on her side.

"Do you read much?" Josie asked.

"I read a lot."

Josie smiled. "I'm a writer."

"That is what Tom said. I'll have to look up your work, because I've never heard of you before."

"I'll be happy to send you a book if you tell me what

you like. I've written a little of everything. What are you reading right now?"

"A microbiology textbook about viruses," Tenzin said. "Have to keep up on current events, don't I?"

Duncan Night said, "What current events? What are you talking about? *Is there going to be a biological—*"

"Sleep." Tenzin put a hand over his mouth and the man's head immediately dropped to the side. She let out a slow breath. "That's so much better."

"Too bad we can't do anything about the smell."

Tenzin said, "Yes, but if he smelled better, we'd probably want to drink him."

They looked at each other a moment before they both started laughing.

Tenzin's eyes were a little pink from tears. "No, but really..." She cleared her throat. "I'm kind of hungry."

"Me too." Josie walked over and put a hand on Duncan's neck. "I do wish it was that simple for me, but it never has been. I'm lucky I have Tom. He takes care of me when I'm not myself."

"We need to finish this. I'm sure Ben and your mate are already heading back to our flat. There are only a couple hours before sunrise."

"What do we do with him?" Josie asked.

Asleep, Duncan Night didn't look like the smug arse whose picture in the paper had enraged her. He looked pathetic. Night was getting older and he wasn't aging well. He clearly didn't take care of himself and showed multiple signs of substance abuse. Who knew if he even wrote his own books anymore?

"I'll wipe his memory as much as possible," Tenzin said. "Should we leave him here or on the street?"

"Not here," Josie said. "That would be a rude awakening for whoever comes home eventually."

Just then, Josie wondered how she'd gotten into the apartment in the first place. She often didn't remember details like that. She turned and saw the wooden door propped in the doorway. She must have ripped it from the hinges to get in.

Tenzin pursed her lips. "I'll leave some money to cover that."

"I'll make sure to pay you back. I'm quite rich."

"So am I. But Ben is always shoving paper money in my pockets."

"Sounds like Tom. To be fair, I always forget to carry any."

Tenzin put a wad of hundred-dollar-bills on the coffee table. "That should be enough. Maybe pay Ben back, not me."

"All right."

"I know!" Tenzin said. "There's a hotel right down the street. We'll leave him on the steps. The doorman will find him eventually, and it's not cold outside."

"Good plan. He certainly smells like he's been drinking."

While Tenzin wiped Duncan Night's memory of the previous few hours, Josie walked around the flat, taking note of the random signs of her odd dementia as she found them. The broken door. A half-eaten apple on the table. The refrigerator hanging open with a bottle of wine tipped to the side. She righted it and closed the door. Then she straightened the pillows in the living room and sprayed cleaner over the urine stain her prisoner had left on the hardwood floor. She felt bad about it now that she'd snapped out of the haze of her anger.

"He won't remember anything?"

Tenzin shook her head. "If anything, it'll seem like a very bad dream."

"Good."

Tenzin was watching her with narrowed eyes.

"I hate it," Josie said. "Tom and I make the best of it, but I know I'm not a normal mate. He'll never be able to leave Dublin because it's worse when I'm not at home in my familiar surroundings." She gestured at Night. "Things like this happen. Every time we travel, I have some kind of incident."

"I don't think he cares," Tenzin said. "He just seemed worried about you."

"I need him so desperately," Josie said, angry that tears came to her eyes. "It's not very fair to him, is it?"

"I think you need each other, and there's nothing wrong with that." Tenzin bent next to Duncan and slung his arm over her shoulder. "Now help me move the dead weight and be glad he's not obsessed with muscles like so many American men."

Josie crouched down and helped Tenzin lift the human, then they walked to the door with Duncan Night dragging his feet between them.

Just as they started down the hall, Josie snickered. "You called him dead weight."

"He's lucky we don't like whiskey."

"Yes. Yes, he is."

"Hey! I have an idea. After this, do you want me to fly you back to our place? It'll be a lot quicker than walking."

Josie's heart leapt. "*Yes*. I definitely do."

"You just have to trust that I won't drop you. Which I won't. I like you."

"Thank you. I do trust you not to drop me. I have a feeling that if you wanted to kill me you'd have done it right away."

"I tell that to Ben all the time, and he still doesn't see the logic."

"Humans."

Chapter Nine

Tom walked into Ben's loft expecting to make a flurry of phone calls only to hear female laughter coming from overhead. He ran to the center of the loft. "Josie?"

"Up here, Tom!"

He looked up and his world settled back on its axis. Josie was hanging over the edge of Tenzin's loft, her eyes lit with amusement, smiling at him with her fangs out. "Hello, my handsome monster."

Tom growled, but he couldn't hold back the smile. "Get down here."

"Catch me."

"Always."

She jumped and he caught her. As he always did. As he always would.

Josie kissed him hard, and when she pulled back he was relieved to see teasing humor instead of grief or guilt.

"I'm so sorry," she whispered. "I got a bit away from myself like I do sometimes."

"I know, Josie-girl." He pressed his lips to her temple. "No harm done?"

"No harm done. Are you angry?"

"Never at you."

"I found a new friend. She's lovely and she flies."

Tom glanced up, and Tenzin was floating over them.

She winked and flew back in her loft.

"Well, that's good news," Tom said. "You can never have too many friends. Especially the flying sort."

Tom looked at Ben over Josie's shoulder. The young man tipped his head and disappeared into his office.

"Why don't we head home, Jo? Get safe before the sunrise, eh?"

"You just want to interrogate me in private," she said.

"You know me so well."

❖

"Tell me." He scraped his teeth over her bottom, nipping at the soft flesh before he crawled up her back. "Tell the truth this time."

Josie giggled and made his life perfect. "We... sold him to a carnival. They thought he'd be brilliant as a knife target."

"No."

"We made him dance in the middle of Union Square. The crowd was so impressed they begged him to take his act to Broadway and he left writing behind."

"Not believing a word." He hadn't taken a stitch of his own clothes off. No, he'd just stripped her naked and tossed her on the bed to begin his "interrogation."

Josie couldn't stop laughing. "We put him on a train to Omaha."

"Now why would you do that to the fine people of Omaha?"

"You're right, that would be cruel." Josie arched up and rubbed her bottom against his hips. "But not as cruel as you."

"Tell me the truth."

She fell back into the pillows. "But Tom, I lie for a living! Why would you ask me to tell you the truth when a story is so much more entertaining?"

He chuckled. "Tell me."

"We lectured him about his horrendous adverb abuse, then left him at the top of the Statue of Liberty to think about what he'd done to a perfectly innocent part of speech!"

Tom paused. Okay, not on her own, but with Tenzin... He caught the glint in her eye as she watched him over her shoulder.

"Nope." He slapped her bottom. "Still not buying it."

Josie flipped over and reached for him. "If you're not going to believe any of my stories, it's going to be a very long night."

Tom crawled up and nibbled on the soft skin of her neck. "I certainly hope so."

Just before dawn, Josie nestled against him, her skin pressed against his, his amnis covering her in warmth and comfort as they drifted toward their day rest.

"Tell me," he whispered.

Her voice was barely audible. "I don't remember how I took him. I was in an empty apartment. I didn't hurt him. I scared him. By the time I found myself again, I couldn't remember what had made me so angry. Tenzin found me just as I was starting to panic."

"She wiped his memory?"

"Yes."

"Then no harm done." He kissed the top of her head.

"Sleep, Josie."

"Tenzin said he won't remember anything, though I'm hoping he might remember at least a little of the writing advice I gave him, because he really needs it."

He smiled so wide, he thought his cheeks might crack. "I'm sure."

"I'm serious, Tom. People won't stop buying his books, so something must be done."

"We'll talk about it more tomorrow."

"Okay."

He felt it when the sun slipped over the horizon. Felt the heaviness in his bones like a weighted blanket settling over him. He was safe in his own room with his mate next to him.

He was complete.

Josie whispered, "I'm sorry."

"For what?"

"I'm sorry I'm not normal, Tom."

"Normal?" He wrapped his other arm around her. "Sweet girl, where would be the fun in that?"

THE END

Dear Readers,

I hope you enjoyed this short visit with Tom and Josie, one of my absolute favorite couples in the Elemental World. When I decided to release *A Very Proper Monster* in a stand-alone edition, I knew I wanted to include something new for readers who wanted to revisit these characters. This idea quickly sprang to mind. I hope you enjoyed seeing them again! I know I enjoyed writing "Night in the Waking City." I hope in the future that Josie whispers to me again.

Thanks for reading,
Elizabeth Hunter

ELIZABETH HUNTER is a contemporary fantasy, paranormal romance, and paranormal mystery writer. She is a graduate of the University of Houston Honors College and a former English teacher. She once substitute taught a kindergarten class but decided that middle school was far less frightening. Thankfully, people now pay her to write books and eighth graders everywhere rejoice.

She currently lives in Central California with her son, two dogs, many plants, and a sadly empty fish tank. She is the author of the Elemental Mysteries and Elemental World series, the Cambio Springs series, the Irin Chronicles, and other works of fiction.

ALSO BY ELIZABETH HUNTER

Made in the USA
Middletown, DE
18 December 2020

29098949R00116